*I saw you first, Jack. You were supposed to be mine.*

He exhaled, broke free, leaned his forehead to hers and whispered, "It's been a long time coming."

She sighed, secretly thrilled he'd missed kissing her. "It was definitely worth the wait."

"I don't know about the wait, but it was pretty damn spectacular on my end," he said, grinning.

She made a breathy laugh, still floating from his kiss.

Dear Reader,

Welcome to Whispering Oaks, a small, tightly knit community in a rural section of Southern California, and the home of the Grady family. Anne is the oldest sibling, who left home shortly after high school to pursue her RN degree and to start a new life far away from the memories that haunted her. A tragic accident brings her home to care for her parents and opens a Pandora's box of emotions.

In *Courting His Favorite Nurse,* Jack Lightfoot has never forgotten his runaway friend, and upon her return, hopes to set the record straight.

Sometimes life throws us more than we can handle, and when Anne and Jack found themselves losing a close friend to illness in high school, neither handled it well. Thirteen years later they get a second chance to resume their old friendship, but Anne still wants to run away, and this time Jack is determined not to let her.

I don't know about you, but I love reunion stories. Won't you join me in Whispering Oaks to see how this one turns out?

I'm thrilled about my debut Harlequin Special Edition, and would love to hear what you think. You can contact me at my website, www.lynnemarshall.com, or by mail at P.O. Box 51, Simi Valley, CA 93062.

Best regards,

Lynne Marshall

# COURTING
# HIS FAVORITE
# NURSE

*LYNNE MARSHALL*

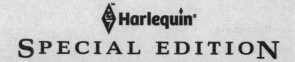

**Harlequin**

**SPECIAL EDITION**

Recycling programs
for this product may
not exist in your area.

ISBN-13: 978-0-373-65660-8

COURTING HIS FAVORITE NURSE

This edition published by arrangement with Harlequin Books S.A.

For questions and comments about the quality of this book please contact us at Customer_eCare@Harlequin.ca.

® and TM are trademarks of Harlequin Books S.A., used under license. Trademarks indicated with ® are registered in the United States Patent and Trademark Office, the Canadian Trade Marks Office and in other countries.

www.Harlequin.com

**Printed in U.S.A.**

**Books by Lynne Marshall**

Harlequin Special Edition

*Courting His Favorite Nurse* #2178

Medical Romance

*Her Baby's Secret Father*
*Her L.A. Knight*
*In His Angel's Arms*
*Single Dad, Nurse Bride*
*Pregnant Nurse, New-Found Family*
*Assignment: Baby*
*Temporary Doctor, Surprise Father*
*The Boss and Nurse Albright*
*The Heart Doctor and the Baby*
*The Christmas Baby Bump*

Other titles by Lynne Marshall available in ebook format.

## *LYNNE MARSHALL*

used to worry that she had a serious problem with day-dreaming—then she discovered she was supposed to write those stories! A late bloomer, Lynne came to fiction writing after her children were nearly grown. Now she battles the empty nest by writing stories that always include a romance, sometimes medicine, a dose of mirth, or both, but always stories from her heart. She is a Southern California native, a dog lover, a cat admirer, a power walker and avid reader.

Special thanks to Jo for getting my feet in the door,
to Gail for giving me a chance and to Sarah
for helping me make this book all it could be.

## Chapter One

"I'm glad you're here, Annie belle," Kieran Grady still sounded groggy from yesterday's surgery. He seemed too big for the hospital bed with his long legs nearly hanging over the end of the frame, the left with a hip-to-foot cast elevated on three pillows.

"I'm glad I'm here, too, Dad." Anne patted her father's hand, making sure his IV was in place and infusing well. An RN for eight years, she couldn't help herself.

"Take care of your mom until I get home," he said, drifting closer to sleep.

"Of course I will," she whispered. Good thing she could get the time off from her new job until Lucas got officially discharged from the army.

Anne's cell phone vibrated in her pocket. She

glanced at the screen. "That's the E.R., Dad. Mom must be ready to go home."

With eyes closed, he nodded.

There was also a text message from Lark: How are Mom and Dad doing? Give them kisses from me. Wish I could be there, but school is crazy! Love you guys. :) No way would anyone expect her sister to leave medical school midsemester when Anne and her brother Lucas could be there for their parents. She texted back: They're fine. I'll call you later.

She bent to kiss her dad's forehead avoiding the scratches and one nasty-looking laceration near his receding hairline. "This one is from me, and this is from Lark."

He smiled then grimaced. "I swear," he mumbled. "I never saw that car coming."

Considering her parents had been on a motorcycle, things could have been a whole lot worse. As an RN she'd seen plenty of motorcycle accident fallouts first-hand, and she didn't approve of his "hobby" but there was no way her father would give up his Harley. And up until now, Mom was as gung ho about their Sunday rides on the open roads as he was. Anne had a hunch Mom might be singing another tune from now on.

Anne said goodbye to her father and his nurse, making sure the RN had her cell number as well as her family's home phone, then headed toward the elevator leaving the plaster and disinfectant scent of the orthopedic ward behind.

She'd arrived in California early the next morning

from Portland, Oregon, but had still missed their surgeries. She'd found the first available flight out the moment she'd been contacted by the E.R. nurse Sunday night. Adrenaline had burst from the center of her chest and tingled out to her fingers and toes at the news. They could have been killed. Oh, God, she couldn't bear to think about the pillars in her life falling…and thankfully, their injuries would heal. Not soon enough for Dad, she thought, smiling and shaking her head as the elevator descended down to the first floor.

After arriving in Whispering Oaks in time for her mother's hospital discharge that morning, she'd taken her home. By midafternoon, when Mom said the pain was excruciating, she'd realized her mother's full arm cast had pressed on a nerve and she was losing sensitivity in her fingers. Anne had turned right around and brought her back to the E.R. to have it removed and a new cast applied before there was a chance for nerve damage.

The small Whispering Oaks hospital overflowed with patients, and they'd spent the better part of the evening waiting. When the orderly wheeled off her mother to the cast room, she'd gone to visit her father in the ortho ward.

Anne got off the elevator as an ambulance siren blared in the distance. She approached the emergency reception desk noting that every chair in the waiting room was filled. A TV monitor droned on with some reality show that only a few people, besides the desk clerk, paid attention to.

"My mother's ready for discharge," she said. "Beverly Grady?"

The distracted receptionist tore away her gaze from the TV long enough to check her list then, without saying a word or offering a smile, she reached under the desk and pressed a buzzer which opened the door to the department.

Anne rushed to her mother's E.R. cubicle.

"How's your father?" Beverly blurted out the moment Anne entered. With a twisted waistband on her teal workout pants, and one sleeve of the jacket hanging over her shoulder, her mother looked out of character from her usual jeans and trendy jerseys approach to style. But Mom wouldn't let Anne bring her to the hospital without makeup and her earrings, the large gold hoops now tangled in her shoulder-length hair, her bright lipstick half chewed off.

"He's doing well, Ma. The nurses say he'll be home in a few days."

"Great news. Why did it have to be my right arm? I'm useless with my left hand. How am I going to take care of him or do my hair or put on makeup?" She shook her head, her layered, bottle brown hair bobbed along. "Do you have any idea how hard it is to hook a bra with one hand?"

"That's why I'm here, remember?" Anne stifled her smile.

Beverly pursed her lips, brows raised, looking impish. "See the extreme some parents will go to just to get their daughter home?"

Anne shook her head and smiled. "An invitation would have been fine."

Beverly swiped the air with her one good arm. "You always have excuses." Her mother laughed wryly, and Anne joined her, avoiding thoughts better left unspoken once again.

"But you and Dad liked visiting Portland." Other than one Christmas three years ago, Anne hadn't returned to Whispering Oaks since she'd gone off to college to get her nursing degree. And that Christmas visit had been mainly because Lucas had gotten a leave for the holidays. It wasn't because she didn't love her parents, no; she loved them with all her heart. It was the guilt and bad memories that seemed to overshadow everything else about her hometown whenever she ventured back.

"But this is your home, Annie."

Truth was, Portland felt more like home these days, she just didn't have the nerve to tell her mother that.

A shrill siren grew closer, soon coming to an abrupt halt outside the rear of the emergency department.

A frazzled looking nurse appeared at their cubicle with dark smudges beneath her eyes, some form of updo gone askew and a wheelchair. "Ready to go?"

Doors flew open at the back of the E.R. and a group of firemen wheeled in a couple people on gurneys. The nurse shot a quick glance over her shoulder, then pushed the wheelchair inside, back to business as usual. Out of reflex from her old E.R. days Anne tensed, but reminded herself she was a clinic nurse now, and that today she was on the patient side of the hospital equation. It felt so different, and yet her curiosity about the latest intake wouldn't back down.

Anne took a quick look at her mother's fingers, pressed the nail beds to make sure the capillaries blanched and pinked right back up. "Can you move your fingers?" she asked over the ruckus.

"Annie, this feels a hundred times better than the last cast."

"Okay then, we're ready to go." Anne gave an assuring smile to the nurse.

She helped her mother into the chair and, after signing the discharge papers, began to roll her toward the exit.

"Keep that cast elevated," the nurse said as she rushed off toward the new patients on the gurneys. So much for patient discharge education.

Across the department a male figure caught Anne's eye. He stood, legs planted in a wide stance, arms folded, just apart from the health care workers and firemen team huddle.

"There's my hero," her mother called out. Then to Anne she said, "Jack was the first on scene Sunday at the accident."

Jack? As in Jackson Lightfoot?

In a whiplash response, Anne turned toward the man just as he noticed her. A thousand crazy thoughts barged into her head as she peered at an apparition. What in the world was he doing here? She blinked as the ghost of heartbreak past came into full view.

Except he looked so much better than that high school jock she'd remembered. As if that were possible. He wore the standard fireman navy blue T-shirt and slacks—without the yellow rubber pants and suspenders—shiny work boots and a serious expression. His blond hair was shorter and darker, and all traces of boyish features were gone. It'd been twelve years, and he still set off a spark in her chest—a feeling so foreign, it felt more like anxiety.

"Mrs. Grady, what are you doing back here?" he said to her mother, though his gaze had found and stuck to Anne.

"Annie said I needed a new cast." She attempted to lift the heavy, hot pink, fiberglass-covered arm.

Anne wished she could disappear behind the nearest cubicle curtain, but Jack stared at her and offered a tentative smile, the kind that only lifted half of his mouth.

"Anne."

She nodded, fighting off the rush of feelings blindsiding her. Nerves zinged, blood rushed to her face and her legs, perfectly stable and strong a moment before, felt unsteady. She was thirty but had taken the fast track back to high school insecurity. "Hey, Jack. Hi." At a loss for what to do or say, and trying desperately to act composed, she went for inane. "Are you a fireman?"

"I volunteer a couple times a week."

His chest had broadened and bulked up since she'd last seen him, and his voice had dropped half a scale.

He'd definitely turned into the man that swaggering eighteen-year-old had hinted at.

He bent and hugged her mother. "How's the old man doing?"

"Fine, thanks to you and your quick thinking. The doctor told Annie, he'll be home in a couple days, come and see him."

"I will." Jack glanced back at Anne, and before she could prepare herself, he hugged her. Granted it was nothing more than one of those awkward pat-the-back deals, but it still rattled her. Even though she'd stiffened up, warm fuzzies hopped along her skin and she wanted to swat at them and yell, *stop it, stop it!*

*Well what do you know, he still uses Irish Spring.*

She leaned back and noticed a lingering fluster in his eyes that she assumed mirrored her own, and a warm, welcoming expression on his face. Man, he still had a great smile, except now it had parentheses around it, and his eyes, those fern green eyes she could never forget, had the beginning of fan lines at the corners making him all the more enticing.

*No. Stop it right now. We already know how this story plays out, and it has a sucky ending.*

"Well, looks like they need some help. It's good to see you, Anne. Beverly, you take care of yourself. I'll visit Kieran tomorrow after school."

"He'll be glad to see you," Beverly said.

And he was off to assist the other firemen with the patient transfers from their gurneys to E.R. beds.

She knew he was a teacher at Whispering Oaks, but when had he gotten so chummy with her parents?

Bursts of memories hijacked Anne's thoughts as she rolled her mother to the car. How after Jack had been her friend first, she'd introduced him to her best friend and lost him. Soon being relegated to the third-wheel buddy role, she'd been forced to watch their budding romance bloom and keep her feelings to herself. And later, how the three of them had gone through the toughest time of their lives together. How he'd become her secret hero, the one she had loved with all her heart...but could never have...unless she betrayed her best friend. The details tangled in a knot between her brows.

"Jack teaches with your father at the high school, you know," Beverly said, while transferring from wheelchair to car. "English and basic mathematics."

"Yes, you have mentioned that a time or two, Mom." How many times had he counted down the days until he'd graduate high school? Now, apparently, he went back on a daily basis.

Beverly went quiet, and Anne understood why. Though Anne had never discussed her heartache with her mother, it would have been impossible for Beverly not to sense the pain back then. It didn't take a genius to figure out who had caused it. She closed the car door and pushed the wheelchair to a collection center then got into the driver's seat.

Shortly after Anne had left Whispering Oaks behind, Jack had, too. Occasionally he'd send a postcard from somewhere around the world, a weak attempt at staying in touch. If he'd felt the way he'd sworn he did—*you're the one, Anne*—why hadn't he ever come after her? Eventually, the cards quit coming altogether.

How many times would she drive herself crazy trying to figure it all out? She started the engine, eager to get away from the hospital with the huge yellow fire rescue vehicle parked in front.

Jackson Lightfoot had been the reason she'd left home, and was the last person on earth she wanted to see now that she was back.

The next afternoon at school, dubbed Sleepless Wednesdays by his students thanks to his Tuesday night volunteer status, Jack nodded off. His chin rebounded off his chest and snapped his head against the chair. The students' tittering dashed any hope that no one had noticed.

"Okay, anyone ready to read their essay out loud?"

That brought the sudden and needed silence he'd hoped for. Maybe he should have refilled his Best Teacher in the World mug with more coffee after lunch.

As everyone went back to work, he tapped the eraser end of a pencil on his desk and thought about Anne. He couldn't help himself. Heck, a toddler could have pushed him over using a pinky finger when he'd first seen her last night.

She'd challenged him to be better from the very first time she'd met him, and in the E.R., he could still see the summons there in her eyes. Those brown eyes the exact shade of her shoulder-length hair. He was glad she hadn't fiddled with the color like so many women did these days. He'd always liked the natural sheen and what he could only describe as the nutmeg color. She'd matured…in a good way. In high school she'd been a little too bony for his type. Now she'd added a few pounds and had smoothed out all the angles.

He laughed inwardly. Her *bod* wasn't what had always attracted him to her. It was her straightforward approach. Her honesty. He scrubbed his face and remembered the day she'd first spoken to him at track practice in eleventh grade.

*"You're full of it, Lightfoot," she'd said. "You've been letting everyone think you're part Native American, but you're name's either English or German. I looked it up."*

*No girl had ever challenged him before. He'd swaggered up to her and glared right into her face. From her unwavering stare, he knew she'd seen through his bravado.*

*Though Lightfoot made a great name for Whispering Oaks' top league hurdler, and having people think he had Native American ancestors made it even cooler, he was as white bread as they came, and she'd called him out on the prevarication.*

*"I'll pay you ten bucks to keep that to yourself."*

*"I don't take bribes, but I'm good with secrets."*

Boy was she ever good with secrets. A week to the day *before* Brianna, his girlfriend and Anne's best friend, had been diagnosed with leukemia, he'd let slip a huge secret to Anne—how he felt about her. And to make matters worse, he'd kissed her. They'd been horsing around after watching a *Star Trek* DVD one Saturday night at her house. Bri hadn't been feeling well and he'd taken her home early. Looking back he should have realized Bri hadn't been feeling well for a few weeks, but he'd been oblivious, even looked forward to spending some time alone with Anne. What a jerk he'd been.

After the movie, imitating Captain Kirk and Spock, he'd placed splayed fingers on Anne's face and asked, "May I join your mind?" Good sport, as always, she had giggled but let him and he'd sworn she'd communicated one thing through those soft doe eyes—kiss me.

*So he did. Jack pressed his mouth to Anne's in a tender first-kiss fashion. Her lips were soft and moist, just as he'd expected. She didn't pull back, but she went still. He shouldn't push things, what about Bri? Ignoring that thought, he kept kissing Anne, eager to explore more, though taking things slow, he felt her shoulders relax.*

*Anne's hands pressed against his chest, a signal to stop, but not before she kissed him back. Jack broke it off searching her eyes for a clue, and saw a mix of shock and held-back longing.*

*"We shouldn't have done that," she said, with a breathy whisper, her nostrils flaring faintly.*

*"I'm sorry." Was he really sorry he'd shared the sweetest kiss since junior high with Anne? He was positive there was something between them just waiting to be unlocked. He knew she felt it, too.*

"She's my best friend." Her hand flew to her mouth, as if to erase the kiss.

He stared at the floor. "You probably don't think much of me as a boyfriend."

"Right now, I don't know what to think."

"I better leave," he said, refusing to regret what they'd done. He'd shaken her up, felt the pull between them. It wasn't his imagination.

Their kiss had been loaded with potential—he couldn't get it out of his mind all weekend and, on Monday he'd seized the moment.

*Jack spotted Anne between classes, heading for the science building. He swept in before she noticed him, grabbed her wrist and tugged her behind the ancient oak tree in the center of the campus. He'd thought about doing this all weekend, no matter how rotten an idea it was. He needed to kiss her again.*

*Like a man possessed, he leaned her against the gnarly bark, hands on her shoulders, and kissed her full-out. Firm and deep, he explored the lips he'd thought about for two days. She dropped her books, and once again she matched him kiss for kiss.*

*Once he'd planted the kiss he'd dreamed about, and only because he heard some howls and comments from other students, he let up.*

*He would have been damned proud of that kiss, seeing her dazed and breathless, pupils dilated, eyes wide, but confusion distracted him. Shame edged its way in. How was he supposed to handle this? Damned if he'd apologize for doing what he'd wanted for months, he said something he shouldn't have and walked away.*

A week later Brianna's mysterious illness got a diagnosis and it turned their world upside down. Nothing else seemed to matter. Anne had never mentioned their kisses again. Under the circumstances he sure as hell wasn't about to bring them up, and their easygoing friendship had never been restored.

Honor mixed with guilt and disappointment could make a guy do crazy things, like after Bri died, he took off in the opposite direction for Europe instead of heading to Oregon to where Anne was. And life had a way of throwing those mistakes in your face. He'd lost his good buddy Anne, the girl with all the possibilities, and he hadn't come close to falling in love with anyone since.

There were a million things he'd like to talk to Anne about, but he didn't have a clue how or where to start. He knew he owed her an apology for the crazy mixed messages he'd given her, and for that bomb he'd dropped just before Bri had died. And if her reaction to seeing him was any indication, he wasn't sure she was the least bit interested in seeing him again.

Jack grimaced and noticed a couple students with raised eyebrows watching him deep in his battling thoughts. He homed in on the ringleader—a girl whom he suspected had a crush on him.

"Amy, are you ready to read your essay?" He used his benevolent teacher voice, the kind that usually got good results. She shook her head with hummingbird speed.

All curious gazes went back to the desks.

After he visited Kieran Grady that afternoon in the hospital, maybe he'd pay a visit to Beverly…and Anne.

"Lucas, we understand. You'll get home as soon as you can. What's a few more days?" Anne said, sitting at her mother's bedside mindlessly running her toes over the dog's bristly brown coat. Lucas was undergoing some army discharge testing in Washington, D.C., and kept extending his ETA. "Dad's doing as well as can be expected considering how banged up he is. I talked to him yesterday and I'll go see him tomorrow. Mom's doing fine, too. She's resting right now. You want to talk to her?"

Beverly lay sprawled on her bed, pink-casted arm elevated above her heart on pillows, and with Bart, her rescued Rhodesian Ridgeback who was too big for the bed, laying dutifully on the rug. With the body of a boxer on steroids and a face more in line with a lab, he was one good-looking doggie, and the newest family addition since their official empty nest.

"I don't want to wake her," Lucas said.

He'd been evasive whenever the topic of conversation turned to how he was doing. The last few times they'd spoken, Anne had gotten the impression he wasn't being completely honest about something. "She's not really asleep. Here she is," Anne said, gently pressing her mother's shoulder.

"Anne!"

She smiled at the sound so clear in her mind. Lucas's tone had transported her back in time.

"It's Lucas." She handed the phone to her sleepy mother, whose face brightened at the sound of her son's name.

Also leaving home right after high school, her brother had completed nine years in the army and, resisting the constant carrot they dangled to keep the medics re-upping, he would finally be discharged in a couple weeks. Thank heavens. Lucas had seen more desert and suffering than he'd ever dreamed, and now would come home to yet another mess—Mom and Dad fresh out of a motorcycle-versus-car accident and both in casts. Comparatively speaking, it should be a walk in the park.

A light tapping pulled Anne out of the room and down the hall toward the kitchen door. And out of pure nosiness Bart's paws clacked down the hall behind her. When she opened it, someone stood behind a huge, colorful bouquet.

"Mrs. G., how are you?" Anne recognized the squeaky voice and grinned. Jocelyn Howard peeked around the corner and beamed from the other side of the flowers. "Annie, when did you get home?"

"Monday." They gave an ardent but awkward hug with the huge vase between them, as a warm homey feeling crept over Anne. When she'd left Whispering Oaks, she'd never wanted to come back, but she'd forgotten all the wonderful people who still lived here.

How often did she get greeted in Portland with such genuine enthusiasm? "Come on, mom's down in her room."

Holding the vase and flowers didn't prevent Jocelyn from greeting Bart, and he made a happy humming sound from the attention.

Jocelyn had lived next door to the Gradys her entire life and felt like an honorary member of the family. She'd been like a little sister to Anne before Lark had been born, had been Lucas's first play pal until he'd started kindergarten and left her behind for boys.

They reached the bedroom just as Beverly hung up the phone.

Taller than average, Jocelyn, with her long legs and slim runner's body, leaned over the bed and kissed Anne's mother. Her straight, light brown hair veiled her pointy profile. "Oh, Mrs. Grady, I'm so sorry to hear about your accident. Anything you need, you just let me know."

"You are such a dear." Beverly kissed her and patted her arm. "Oh, look at those gorgeous flowers!"

"They're from my mom's rose garden." Jocelyn set them on the bedside table next to the window. The waning March sun barely reached the peach and cranberry colored petals, but their potent scent invaded Anne's nostrils in a burst. They reminded her of her new home, Portland, The City of Roses, and she wondered how the medical clinic was doing without her.

"I'm serious. I'm right next door. If you need an extra pair of hands or some caregiver time off—" She glanced over her shoulder toward Anne. "—I'm glad to help." She poured some water for Beverly, then sat on the edge of her bed and chatted with her. Bart, though wary of the cast, sat at attention and looked on as if he understood every word.

"How's Mr. Grady doing?"

"He's grousing about this accident happening during track season." Anne leaned forward, rubbing Bart's long nose. "You miss your big guy, don't you," she cooed through puckered lips, gazing into earnest brown eyes. He offered his paw. She shook it.

"I don't blame him. We've got a shot at league finals this year." Jocelyn turned to Anne. "Did you know that I'm his assistant coach?"

"You're kidding, since when?" Anne felt out of the loop, with a tinge of hurt. When had her parents quit trying to keep her up on the comings and goings of her hometown? Maybe around the same time she'd stopped showing the least bit of interest?

"Since I transferred from Imperial to Whispering Oaks last year." So Jocelyn had moved back to her alma mater from their crosstown rival school.

"Well, Dad always expected great things from you on that track field. You made up for the poor excuse for athletes Lark and I were."

Jocelyn tilted her head and toed the braided rug on the hardwood floor. "You guys weren't as bad as you think, and Lucas was fast."

"Oh, yeah, he was always good at running *away* from things." Her sisterly dig fell flat. She'd forgotten how Jocelyn had always idolized Lucas, and suspected if he'd paid more attention to her, she would have fallen for him. Probably had anyway. And Anne knew there was nothing worse than unrequited love. Maybe she and Jocelyn had more in common than she realized.

"I was just talking to Lucas," Beverly said.

Jocelyn's lively hazel eyes brightened. "Oh, how's he doing?"

As they chatted on, Anne tossed around a reason to leave the room. Didn't she need to call and update Lark? And maybe she should call work to see how her replacement was doing. There were so many little things she'd forgotten to leave notes about. But the doorbell distracted her, and Bart went on immediate sentry duty. She glanced at her watch and took off down the hall, dog at her heels, prepared to tell whichever solicitor it was, she wasn't interested!

She opened the door with the words "no thank you" on the tip of her tongue. Her mouth dropped along with her stomach at the sight of Jack standing on her door-step.

## Chapter Two

The hair rose on Anne's arms as she stared at Jack who was holding two plastic bags with take-out containers inside. He smiled that straight, white, signature smile. Bart barked once, and pranced excitedly around in a circle as if they were old friends. Traitor.

"I have it on good authority that your mother likes her buffalo wings *hot*." He raised one of the bags.

"Just like her men," Anne repeated her father's favorite line and rolled her eyes. Obviously, Dad wanted to make sure his main squeeze got her favorite meal and Jack was merely a conduit.

Jack grinned and nodded as if he'd been schooled by the master. "Just like her men," he repeated. "Oh, and coleslaw without mayo, which was a little harder to find." He raised the other bag.

"Skinny slaw," she said, at a loss for anything else to say. Her father's sweet gesture made Anne smile even though it had put her in a most uncomfortable position. Should she take the food and close the door? Even by her dodge-the-past-at-all-costs standards, that would be cold.

"May I come in?"

How could she refuse? Anne hated to cook, knew that inevitably Beverly would get hungry, yet hadn't planned or stocked up for a single meal, and something in one of those bags smelled fresh and heavenly.

"Of course," she said, breaking the awkward pause. "Come in." How was she supposed to play this? As if he hadn't broken her heart or helped her betray her best friend? Or as if he was once a great friend whom she'd adored, and had laughed and cried with more than any other person on earth…but who'd drifted away? Still undecided, she scratched her forehead and put on her best hostess face.

She showed Jack to the kitchen where he unloaded the bags on the counter and immediately paid his respects to Bart, who sniffed his hands excited by the scent of chicken. Jack glanced around the room as if recalling being here a thousand times long ago. "Did they remodel?"

Anne nodded. Since she'd moved out, her mother had added French Country flair to their sturdy ranch-style home. They'd knocked down a wall and opened up the flow of the kitchen into the family room. Now they had a block wood island, and trendy glass-fronted white cupboards with granite countertops, and shelves with canisters and spices lining the walls. Plus a state-of-the-art gas stove with a gazillion burners for Beverly's love of cooking, and a two-foot-long tilted rack for all of her international cookbooks. Trying her best to avoid facing Jack, she spotted the perfect place to put Jocelyn's flowers on the antique wood sideboard, deciding to do it later.

"I'll go get my mom," she said, turning, but her mother and Jocelyn were coming to them.

"I could smell the food all the way down the hall. Jack, you shouldn't have," Beverly said, smoothing the pillow's impact on her hair. "But I'm really glad you did."

He wiped his hands on his khaki slacks and shook hers as if he hadn't seen her in months. "I couldn't let the big guy down." He winked at her mother. "He was worried Anne wouldn't fix you dinner or, worse, that she would."

A mischievous glint graced his eyes, and if Anne weren't so busy feeling conspired against, and a bit like an outsider, she might have laughed along with everyone else.

"Har har. Hey, I may be a lousy cook, but I'd never let my mommy go hungry. I remember how to dial for takeout. Was just thinking about doing it, too."

She opened a cupboard and got down some dishes. Beverly insisted on setting the utensils on the table with her one good hand, making several extra trips in the process, Bart dogging her every step. Jocelyn

took drink orders and Jack, well, he stood there looking gorgeous with his late afternoon stubble and super-
starched pale blue pin-striped shirt that hadn't a hint of
a wrinkle.

He must have felt her studying gaze when he used
his thumb to scratch his upper lip and glanced at the
floor.

How was she going to share a meal with him and
act casual? If he subscribed to the popular fallacy that
time healed all wounds, she had some news for him.
She sighed, then took her place at the table, deciding to
beat everyone to the fresh-from-the-oven garlic rolls.

"Why do you volunteer with the fire department?"
Anne had acted more like a journalist than an old friend
throughout dinner. In between her barrage of questions,
all neatly superficial, Jack had noticed she only picked
at her food.

"California's broke. Whispering Oaks depends on
volunteers to make up for the shortage of firemen, and
I guess it's my way of giving back."

Anne didn't need clarification on what he was giving
back for. How many times had Brianna been rushed to
the hospital in an ambulance? The fire department had
been first on scene the day she had collapsed at school,
and at their prom...

"Sort of like the same reason you became a nurse,"
her mother said.

"Brianna," Anne said.

Okay, so she'd go first at naming the elephant in the room.

"Brianna," he repeated just before taking a large swallow of his iced tea.

Her gaze met and held his for the briefest of moments, just long enough to confuse him and make him wish he could read her mind.

Seeing Anne's eyes dance away each time he'd tried to engage them, gave him a clue that it wouldn't be easy to convince her to spend some time with him. Just the two of them. He definitely needed to deliver that apology.

As dinner wound down, Jack decided to go for it, to take the sneaky route and make his move in front of an audience. If he hadn't already committed to meeting the latest in a long string of computer-arranged *compatible-dates.com,* and if he hadn't cancelled on this particular lady before, he would ask Anne out for coffee tomorrow night. Now, he needed to come up with something else, and fast.

"Anne, you feel like going for a hike to Boulder Peak for old time's sake this Saturday morning?" he said, knowing it had once been one of their favorite places to hang out.

She blinked a half dozen times and wiped her mouth before answering. "Oh, that sounds great, but I can't. I'm taking Mom to get her hair and nails done. Right?" His spin ball got deflected with the precision of Venus Williams.

"We can do it another day," Beverly said, a sheepish look in her eyes as she took a dainty bite of wing.

"But you want to look nice when Dad comes home. You told me yourself."

"I can take her," Jocelyn piped in.

The expression on Anne's face could be described as mortified, but Jack decided not to focus on the negative. She could protest all she wanted, but apparently the team was on his side.

He smiled. "Then I'll pick you up at eight."

Friday evening, Anne propped up her mother's arm, made sure everything she could want was within reach, and armed with her mother's long grocery list, she set out to do some shopping. Bart sat in the family room attentively at Beverly's side watching over her.

On the drive home odd tidbits from life elbowed their way into Anne's mind. She drove down familiar streets, each with a memory attached, and having spent so much time with her mother and spoken to both her brother and sister yesterday, everything seemed to invite reflection.

She hadn't minded getting knocked off the pedestal when Lucas had come along. She enjoyed having a brother…at first. Mom kept calling her the "big girl," even though she wasn't sure she liked the new title or what it meant. As Lucas got older, she discovered she could make him laugh, and Mom was happy about that, so she did it a lot. He was a good laugher back then. Now? Not so much.

Though they hadn't seen each other in three years, they occasionally spoke on the phone and emailed back and forth on a regular basis. Lately, Lucas's take on life seemed so cynical, and it worried her. She missed her brother and couldn't wait to see him. Besides, the sooner he got home, the sooner she could go back to Portland and her new job.

She cruised past her old grammar school and its single-story 1950s blah architecture, the place where her mother still taught fourth grade. A thousand more memories crowded her head. How many times had she defended Lucas when he'd gotten into trouble there? Early on they'd teamed up and stayed united when it was apparent Lark could do no wrong. Maybe he could use someone in his corner these days too, and she shouldn't rush off right after he got here.

Coming home put a bittersweet taste in her mouth with so many landmarks holding memories. She drove past the park where she used to play and thought how when Lark came along she'd been five and it felt as if Mom had sent her to school just so she could be alone with her little brother and baby sister.

When Lark was a baby, she had fluffy white hair, and she didn't have to say one word to get Mom and Dad to smile, all she had to do was be there. Anne learned if she read her books out loud, Dad would clap his hands, so she read everything she could find aloud, and knew early on the importance of being a high achiever.

So why was Lark the one in med school?

She huffed a breath and glanced toward the sky. Let it go, Anne. You're thirty and you're an adult. If you want to go to medical school, you can apply. Truth was, she liked being a nurse, and back when she'd taken the MCATs and had scored well, her parents simply didn't have the money or the desire to take out humongous loans. She couldn't blame them. When Lark was ready to apply to college, they owned their home and Dad's Great Aunt Tessa had left him a windfall in her will. If there was one thing Anne had learned, it was that life wasn't fair and timing ruled the day and it was a futile task to try to figure out why anything worked the way it did.

What more proof did she need than her best friend dying shortly after her eighteenth birthday, just before graduating?

She drove past the Whispering Oaks Gymnastics Center, which used to be nothing more than a huge garage with mats, and remembered her mother waiting for her during class. It occurred to her that when her mother was her age, she had already had three kids. Not that Anne wanted three kids, but the possibility of a boyfriend at thirty would be nice. Her dating history had been anything but a success, with the last real relationship ending over a year ago. Somewhere along the line she'd figured her miserable excuse for a love life was likely because somewhere deep inside she still carried a torch for Jack.

Must all thoughts lead back to Jack?

The streets seemed more crowded than when she'd

left, and there were strip malls on far too many corners. There seemed to be fewer trees, too. At least the
surrounding hills hadn't changed. She'd missed them.
In the distance she could see Boulder Peak jutting its
rocky nose above the hilltop, and immediately tried to
divert her thoughts away from the invitation to hike
there. With Jack. Jack. Again, thoughts about Jack.

What would it be like to spend time with him? She'd
much prefer to dodge the whole thing, but everyone had
plotted against her and she'd had no way out. Maybe
she could sprain her ankle between now and tomorrow
morning?

And speaking of Jack, wasn't that him heading into
TGI Fridays with a pert redhead by his side?

She slowed down as she drove past one of the three
main restaurants in town feeling like a stalking teenager. Her heart raced as she looked closer. At least he
wasn't holding the woman's hand. So what was the deal
about asking her to go hiking?

Time marches on and she'd been gone for a while
now, so she couldn't exactly hold a grudge if Jack had
a girlfriend. She groaned over getting swept up in the
crappy moment. Why did she feel like she was in high
school again mooning over the jock that got away?
*Sure, Jack, take the good ol' buddy hiking, buy the
redhead dinner.* Now thoroughly confused, she hit the
gas and headed for the market.

A half hour later, she parked the car in the garage
and entered through the kitchen with the bags,

where Bart met her. "Good boy. Did you take care of mommy?" His tail thumped the nearby counter.

She put everything away, grabbed a bottle of water from the refrigerator and took a swig. Mom was asleep in the recliner in the family room, so she plopped down on the same couch from which she used to watch *Buffy,* glad they hadn't gotten rid of it with the remodel.

Mom had apparently fallen asleep watching some reality show about crab fishermen, and the narrator's voice sounded just like her father's. Loud. Friendly. Baritone. Maybe that's why her mother smiled in her sleep? Anne hoped Dad was getting used to his huge cast and lack of independence. He'd seemed restless and impatient earlier today when she'd visited him, which didn't bode well for when he came home after the weekend.

Something pushed against her back. She pulled it out as she took another drink. Grandma's fancy embroidery decorated a small lacy pillow Anne had seen her entire life: *Good things come to those who wait.*

She wouldn't dare call her grandma corny, but so far the catchy saying hadn't panned out. Her fingers traced the precision stitches.

Just how long was a girl supposed to wait?

The next morning Anne glared at her puffy eyes and sallow complexion. Would Jack notice if she put on some mascara? For hiking? She imagined sweat getting into her eyes and the black smudges under her lids when she rubbed them in the glaring sun. Maybe not.

What would they talk about? Would everything focus around Brianna? She wasn't sure she was ready to talk about her personal life with him, wasn't sure he deserved to know anything. Why had she agreed to go hiking? Oh, right, she'd been bamboozled into it.

If she kept things superficial, she might bore him to death, then maybe he'd leave her alone so she could finally forget him.

*Concentrate on the hiking, Anne. The hiking.*

The doorbell rang. One last pat of her uncooperative hair then she jogged down the hall to answer it. It wasn't Jack, and the disappointment surprised her. Why work up a perfectly good case of jitters for nothing?

Jocelyn greeted her wearing workout gear with a warm-up jacket, her hair in a high bouncy ponytail. They hugged in greeting. "I thought I'd bring Bart along while I walk my dogs."

Bart must have heard his name since he came bounding down the hall, pads slip-sliding around the corner.

"He'd love it!" Anne knelt to get face-to-face with the dog. "You want to walk?" He knew the word and tossed his head in excitement, letting out a dog-styled squeal. "Let me get his leash." By now, he'd worked himself into a frenzy, whining and prancing around in circles.

"I'll help your mom get ready for her appointment when I get back," Jocelyn said as she trotted off with three dogs pulling her down the street.

Anne waved goodbye and watched for a few moments. She smiled then immediately stopped as she caught a glance of Jack's car coming up the tree-canopied street, releasing a new flock of butterflies in her chest. Should she stand there and wait for him to arrive and park, or go back inside? Adrenaline pumped through her veins, another unwanted reminder of what Jack could do to her. If she stood here gawking he'd be able to tell how nervous she was. If she went back inside, she ran the risk of him seeing her and wondering why she didn't wait for him. *Make up your mind, Anne, go inside or wait out here.*

Maybe the most important question was: After all these years, why could Jack still make her act like such a scatterbrain?

## Chapter Three

Jack arrived at Anne's house just before eight with a backpack filled with water and sandwiches, and an unnerving pulse thumping in his chest. White clouds scudded across the soft blue sky thanks to typical Whispering Oaks weather, as spring sunshine warmed his shoulders on the walk to her door. He needed a deep breath to calm down, to put things into perspective. This was just a hike with an old high school friend... whom he'd happened to fall for and put on the spot a long time ago. Hell, no one felt guiltier about that than he did. If he worked things right, maybe today he could broach the subject, and apologize. Maybe, finally, they could start fresh, see where it led.

He knocked three times, and she opened the door as if she'd been standing right on the other side.

"Hi," he said, the sight of Anne forcing him to either jump into action or stand there like a tongue-tied idiot. "Ready for a workout?" he asked, having gone the animated route, sounding more like a male cheerleader than the contrite dude he'd imagined.

"Sure!" Evidently his fake pep was contagious.

Anne looked great in shorts and cross trainers. Her greeting smile competed with the bright sky, and he was extra glad she'd worn her hair down.

She glanced upward. "Looks like a great day for a hike. Hold on a sec while I say goodbye to my mom."

He took the opportunity to give himself a stern talking to. No expectations. Just be yourself, then tell her you're sorry. Sorry about everything.

When she returned, her bubbly façade seemed to have worn off. Had Beverly, with all her good intentions, put too much pressure on her and made this out to be more than a hike? He could only guess. She gave him a solemn glance as she closed and checked the lock on the front door. Putting on her sunglasses she started down the brick pathway to the steps across the lawn. On the walk to the curb, he liked how the sun seemed woven through her nutmeg-colored waves, and was so distracted he almost missed a step. *Dude, get a grip.*

He rushed to open the car door for her. "I guess we've got a lot of catching up to do."

She paused before getting into the car. "I thought we were hiking," she said, and he'd have given a hundred dollars to get a look behind her Hollywood-large sunglasses to try to read this mood shift. His fishing expedition wasn't going to be nearly as easy as he'd hoped. In all honesty, could he blame her?

Suddenly feeling more like being on one of his computer-arranged dates instead of hanging with his old friend, he started with the usual superficial banter as they drove off. "So, how do you like living in Portland?"

"It's great," was all she said, glancing out the passenger window.

"It's a shame about what happened to your parents, huh?"

She sighed. "Thank goodness it wasn't worse."

Could the conversation get any more stilted than this? He decided to back off and see how things played out as he switched on the radio.

Fifteen minutes later, by the time they'd reached the parking area and he hadn't made much headway with breaking Anne's icy barrier, the familiar sight of their old hiking grounds made him grin.

"Remember?" he said, only now realizing how tight his jaw had gotten with her silence.

She nodded, a tentative twitch to her lips that he interpreted as a smile.

He shrugged the backpack over his shoulders. "I've got water if you need it." He tried not to stare at her smooth legs that had shaped up nicely since her track days. "Just holler if you want to take any breaks."

"Sounds good."

He led the way to their favorite trailhead, and they set off.

An hour and minimal conversations later, they'd hiked to the top of Boulder Peak. He'd purposely held back and let nature do the job of loosening up Anne.

From this vantage point, to the east, he could see the overly developed valley suburbs of Los Angeles; to the west, the bedroom community roofs hugging the surrounding foothills. Thanks to some recent rain, there were tufts of green between the boulders. This was the view he'd longed for. This was the special place he, Brianna and Anne had often hiked to.

"I'd forgotten how gorgeous it is up here," Anne said, showing the first signs of her old self, her hair floating on the breeze and covering her cheeks.

She came and stood by him and together they revered the panoramic view for several more seconds. It was clear enough to see sparkles from the ocean far in the distance. This gave him the opportunity to smell her flowery soap or body lotion or whatever it was. All he knew was that he liked it, and he liked having her near.

Jack hated feeling like Anne was a stranger, and so far she hadn't made things easy, so on a whim he grabbed her hand. "Hey, I want to show you something." He tugged her toward another outcropping and around its corner. His eyes scanned the surface of the rock wall until he found it. He used his palm to rub away dust and debris. "Look," he said, pointing to a fading circle with three sets of initials inside—his,

Brianna's and Anne's, and below in tiny letters, *BFF. Best friends forever.*

"I make a point to come up here once in a while, and I found this last year." He stood smiling at the names, completely aware how close by Anne was.

"She had a great smile, didn't she?" Anne removed her sunglasses so she could wipe her brightening eyes.

"She did," he said, flushed with mixed-up feelings about the woman standing next to him fighting off tears.

"I think it's great that you come here. She deserves not to be forgotten, you know?"

His throat tightened. "I don't get the same feeling when I visit her grave. It's just a plot. But here, we have memories, don't we?" He didn't want to come off foolish, not after all these years. Not to Anne. So he swallowed against the emotion balling in his chest. God, he'd made a mess of things back then, but how could he have known what was about to happen to Brianna?

The sun made Anne's eyes glisten as she looked on the verge of crying. This wasn't what he'd intended, he didn't want to wallow in sadness, not with Anne. They'd already lived through enough of that for a lifetime, and right now a change in mood was in order. "For being such a great cheerleader, she sure was a klutz, wasn't she?"

Anne blurted out a laugh and it brought a rush of relief. "Remember the time she got so excited cheering you on at league finals that she fell over the railing?"

The snapshot in time, so clear of him sprinting for

the finish line, seeing Bri jumping and screaming then flipping over the bar and landing on her butt right on the track, made him bark a laugh. Anne joined him as the welcomed laughter broke down another barrier between him and his old friend.

He tossed her a bottle of water and opened one for himself. They drank and smiled at each other, the first genuine smile of the day. It felt great.

"Remember the cave?"

She nodded, leading the way to their favorite hiding place. Fifteen minutes later, on another peak with an equally gorgeous view, they entered the shallow cave. Sheltered from the sun and constant wind, he sat on a rock with his feet propped on another. She sat across from him on another outcrop, and he tossed her a granola bar.

"How do you like teaching?" she asked.

"I never thought I'd say this, but I really like it."

"When did you go back to school?"

"Long story."

"I'm interested. Tell me," she said taking a bite.

He wasn't about to shut her down after it had taken so long to get her to loosen up. Maybe if he went first, she'd tell him something about herself.

"Okay, then. First, I kicked around Europe for a while. I found jobs where people paid me under the table, then I hired on as a deckhand on an American yacht in Italy and sailed around the Mediterranean and wound up in Greece but I couldn't find any work, and I couldn't speak the language, so when my money ran out, I had to come home." He chewed the last of his granola bar. "My dad wouldn't let me freeload, so I got a job at Starbucks and went to school to become an EMT."

"You were a barista?"

"A damn good one, too. Remind me, and I'll make you a mocha cappuccino sometime."

She gave a smile that took him right back to high school, a smile that included a taste of challenge. He'd missed that look more than he'd realized.

He got out an apple, rubbed it on his shirt and took a bite. As an afterthought, he held up the second apple for Anne's inspection. She cupped her hands so he tossed it to her, and she bit right in.

"Go on," she said, her mouth full of apple.

"Hitting the books put the bug in me to go back to school, and while I worked as an EMT in the day I went to night school at Marshfield City College." He took another bite of apple and swig of water. "Long story short, I transferred to CSUCI the first year it opened. We called it *sushi* back then. Anyway, I got my teaching credential four years later. I lucked into a job at WO High a couple years ago. Had a horrendous commute to West L.A. before that."

"That's great, Jack." Anne looked genuinely interested, and he figured he'd ride the crest of his opening up in hopes of getting her to talk.

"So how do you *really* like living in Portland?"

She smiled at his obvious swipe at her earlier tight-lipped response. "I love it. It's a gorgeous city. Very eco-friendly. Warm dry summers and rainy winters. Clean air."

She handed him her apple core and he put it inside a plastic baggie along with his own. "What about your job?"

"It's great. I just started a new job last month as the lead nurse for fourteen doctors in a clinic practice. It's very different from hospital work, part administrative and part hands-on medicine, but overall a lot less stressful." She grew pensive and he worried she'd shut down again. "Lately, I've been thinking of going back to school."

"For what?"

She avoided his laser stare and fiddled with a tiny yellow flower on a tall mustard weed. "I don't know, I'm still thinking about it."

She hadn't really opened up about anything, so he thought he'd take a circular route to getting to what he was most curious about. "Do you have a roommate?"

She shook her head, still engrossed with the flower. "I lease a tiny apartment in the Pearl District. It's a great area, loads of things to do, and I can walk almost everywhere. It's fairly close to my job, too."

Maybe she really was happy there. From the glint in her eyes as she went on about her neighborhood, he sensed she'd found a home for good. The realization sat like a boulder in his apple-filled stomach. Hadn't the last thing he'd said to her before she had left Whispering Oaks been something like, *moving on doesn't necessarily mean you're moving forward.* It hadn't been the case for him, but for her maybe it had. An aching sense of loss made him blurt out the next question.

"You seeing anyone?"

Her brows lifted then drew together. She stared at her knees. "Uh, no." The twist to her lips could only be described as a smirk. "Not this year, anyway."

On a breath of air, he relaxed. "I hear ya," he said with a mixed rush of relief and possibilities. "I've resorted to computer dating, myself."

Her interest piqued, she slanted a sideways glance his way. "How's that working for you?"

He shrugged. "Let's just say, I'm not sure dating should be a science."

That got a laugh out of her, and he decided to not try to explain how something was always missing, though on paper he and his computer dates had seemed well matched. He couldn't figure out a lot of things these days, like the heightened desire to find a compatible partner, and the constant disappointment with his dates. "What do you say we take the dome?"

"Today?"

"It's only ten. We can head up there and eat lunch then I promise to take you right home."

She flashed her signature challenging look. "I'll race you to the top!" And she was off before he could get his backpack over his shoulders.

"That's not fair, speedy!" He resorted to taunting her with the nickname he'd given her in high school for always finishing last in the 800M race. She laughed and her feet stuttered on loose gravel. Anne grabbed a root sticking out of a rock to steady her and glared over her shoulder. It wasn't a real glare, but one of Anne's pretend angry looks, and it took him right back to high school and that girl he used to know. Now he was getting somewhere.

The drive home was companionably quiet. Anne couldn't help but think Jack had something else he wanted to say. The muscle worked at the corner of his jaw, his hand gripped the steering wheel harder than necessary. Why did she have the compulsion to run her fingers through the close cropped dark blond waves on his head? Instead, she sighed and looked out the passenger window.

When he pulled into her driveway, he threw the car into Park and turned toward her. "You remember Drew?"

She nodded. Drew had been Jack's best friend in high school. Evidently they were still close.

"He's got his own hot air balloon company right over in Marshfield. I used to work for him on weekends and during the summers when I went to CSUCI. Why don't you let me take you up for a ride next Saturday? You can't say you've really seen Whispering Oaks until you've seen it from the air."

She ignored the charming glint in those fern green eyes.

The thought of floating in the air hanging in a basket with Jack had its merits, but last night, when she couldn't fall asleep, she'd promised not to fall back into their old pattern of being the odd man out with Brianna at the center. And a lot of today had been about Bri. Of course Brianna deserved it, and it was a good starting off place for her and Jack to try to sort things out from before, but everything still seemed so confusing. And how much guilt could she take with Brianna's memory breathing over her shoulder reminding her how she'd betrayed her best friend by loving Jack, by stealing his attention when Brianna was getting sick and no one even knew it.

*I think Jack likes someone else, she'd told Anne over the phone the week before the diagnosis.*

If she was still this messed up over their situation, how must Jack feel?

Anne glanced at Jack and got the distinct impression he needed to spend time with her. She'd worked with grieving families as a nurse, and recognized his need for closure. And God only knew how much needed to be closed, but didn't she have enough on her plate with her mom and dad? And, really, what was the point? They weren't involved in each other's lives anymore.

"Jack, it's been great seeing you again. I really enjoyed the hike today, but I'm here to take care of my parents. I'm afraid I'll have to pass."

He didn't try to hide his disappointment. "You? Afraid?"

"What?"

"You said, 'I'm afraid I'll have to pass' but what I heard was 'I'm afraid'. You've never been afraid of anything, Anne."

She tossed him a disbelieving glance. "You sure we're talking about the same person?"

He shrugged. "That's how I've always seen it."

Was that a challenge in his eyes? Was it finally time to see if those embers of interest were still ignitable? Maybe where Jack was concerned she *was* afraid, and she definitely didn't want to deal with these mixed-up guilty thoughts. Not now. Not under these circumstances. He'd put her through hell. She'd left town because of him—well that and college. And hadn't she seen him with another woman last night, computer date or not! Why set herself up for more heartache? Besides, once Lucas got home, she was leaving. Again. She *had* moved on.

"Thanks for the vote of confidence, but I've got to go inside," she said as she opened the car door.

"You'll burn out if you're not careful." He wasn't making it easy, but she closed the door anyway. "Call me if you need anything, okay?"

She bent and ducked her head through the window. "Okay. But Jack? You've got to understand that I can't be your buddy anymore."

She bit her bottom lip. Jack used to like her straight-arrow honesty, but from the thoughtful, almost hurt expression on his face, she knew she'd gone too far. Too late. She couldn't take back what she'd already said, and it *was* how she felt.

"That's not what I'm asking," he said, brows low, eyes crinkled and staring at the steering wheel.

"Sorry." She didn't give him the chance to explain

further as she strode up the walkway to her front door and let herself in.

*I can't be your buddy because it hurts too damn much.*

Sunday, Anne and Beverly got confirmation that Kieran would indeed be discharged on Monday. When Anne questioned being able to fit Dad into the family compact sedan, she'd been assured by her father that the transportation home had been prearranged.

Monday afternoon an ancient yet familiar beat-up blue van pulled into the driveway, and once again, in her own home, Anne felt conspired against. She rolled the wheelchair to the sliding door where her father smiled, casted leg extended from one captain seat to the other in the huge belly of the vehicle. Jack sat behind the wheel with a tentative look on his face. It was the first time she'd seen him since she'd slammed him about trying to pick up where they'd left off. At least he didn't look like he hated her.

She nodded at him. He lifted a hand as a wave. "Hold on a minute, let me help," he said, hopping out the door and rounding the van.

Beverly stood behind Anne waving at her husband. "Welcome home, sweetie."

"It's great to be back, babe!"

"I'll take care of this," Jack said, as Anne pushed the wheelchair right to the side of the car. "We worked everything out at the hospital when we loaded him up."

Several minutes passed as Jack and her dad played

the maxi-van version of Twister, but emerged with Dad tottering on crutches just long enough to hop to the wheelchair.

Thinking in advance, Anne had put a sturdy slab of plywood over the two inch step-up through the kitchen door. With arm muscles tight and bulging, Jack pushed the two hundred pounds of her father, plus full leg cast, as if they weighed no more than a Hello Kitty stroller.

Anne tried her best not to watch, but gave in at the first glimpse of his deltoids.

Once inside, Beverly hugged Kieran, smiling until her eyes disappeared. He kissed her on the cheek since she was still smiling. "It's great to be home," he said.

Bart was beside himself with his favorite person back from "gone," and high stepped and whined for attention. "There's my boy," Kieran said, kissing the dog's nose and rubbing his ears. If dogs could smile, Bart was.

"Where should I put him?" Jack asked.

"Over here." Beverly pointed the way to the family room and Jack steered past.

Anne brought in the crutches left leaning against the van, anything to distance herself from Jack and his invasion of her family. When she stepped back into the kitchen, she heard her father ask his favorite question. "What's to eat? Do you have any idea how bad hospital food is?"

Anne opened the refrigerator and got out the pound of deli turkey and horseradish cheddar cheese slices she'd bought in anticipation of her father's homecoming. She'd keep herself busy and let her parents occupy Jack.

She brought the tray of sandwiches to the family room and everyone dug in. Kieran was so happy to be home he tossed a half sandwich to Bart who caught it in midair and swallowed without nearly enough chewing.

Throughout all the activity and chatting, Anne caught glimpses of Jack stealing looks at her. Why did she give him the power to make her nervous? And each time she'd make a sorry attempt at a smile, he did the same. Yet when he left, all he did was wave goodbye. Maybe she'd gotten through to him.

Kieran insisted Jack return the next day after school to help him wash up, refusing to let his daughter, *the nurse* who'd seen *everything*, assist.

Once again faced with Jack, looking fit in well-worn jeans and a T-shirt, her palms tingled, there were tickles behind her knees and a flutter in her chest. She fought off the reactions by pretending to be engrossed in cutting the left leg out of two pairs of sweatpants for her father, and sent Jack down the hall to her father's bedroom. It didn't work. All the way from the family room, she strained to eavesdrop on their conversation over the sound of the running shower, and almost shushed her mother when she insisted on talking.

"Should we ask Jack to stay for dinner?" Beverly asked while attempting to stick a ruler under her cast.

"Mom, stop that. You can get an infection. And no, I was only planning on soup and sandwiches, and I'm sure Jack has other plans."

"He's been a lifesaver."

"And what have I been, Mom?" Feeling overlooked again, Anne made a point of being in the laundry room when Jack left.

Being a twenty-four-hour on-call nurse had nearly wiped out Anne, both physically and mentally. Not that her parents were demanding, but dealing with their dueling casts and cooking—something she loathed but did because her parents wouldn't tolerate frozen food— had all taken its toll. She counted the days until Lucas's return.

Thursday, the laundry got interrupted with a shout.

"Annie belle!" her father's booming but muffled voice called from down the hall.

She rushed to his aid but the door wouldn't open. "Don't come in," her mother said from the other side. Bart paced with concern outside.

Once again, modesty kept father from allowing daughter to help. Not that she could have anyway, without straining her back. "Then why call me?"

"Let me get something to cover him, then you can go in."

Kieran had gotten the bright idea to take a bath with his leg propped up on the side of the tub. He'd log-rolled into the extra long master bath tub using his upper body strength and sheer will, with Beverly, the enabler, on standby. Mom had turned on the water. All had gone well until it was time to get out of the tub.

One look was all it took. "I can't get you out of there."

"Then call Jack," Kieran said.

Anne scrubbed her face and did what she was told, thinking it might take the whole fire department, not just Jack to help her dad.

Soon after, there was Jack again, at her door, looking great in a formfitting brown Henley shirt and smelling fresh from the shower, hair still damp and scented with something spicy. He had every right to plaster that self-satisfied grin on his face. Fortunately, she was too exhausted to care. His warning came back to taunt her, "You'll burn out." Truer words had never been spoken.

A half hour later, after what Anne could only imagine to be an amusing if not slapstick dislodgement of her father from the tub, they emerged with Kieran in the wheelchair, and Jack a bit disheveled, but with a victorious smile on his face. The grin, aimed directly at Anne, nearly knocked her knees from under her.

"You ready for that balloon ride yet, speedy?" he asked, once her parents were distracted.

She had to hand it to him, he was persistent, even after her hurtful outburst the other day. And if she were being honest, she'd admit that it felt pretty darn good to be the object of his attention, too. She couldn't remember the last time a guy, *any guy,* had wanted to spend time with her.

Lifting her palms, she shrugged, looked around at the mess accumulating in the house, and at the two culprits reclining in the family room, each with a cast elevated on pillows, watching cable news. "There's just no way, Jack, but thanks for thinking of me."

He used his thumb to scratch his upper lip, then bid her parents good-night. She expected him to head for the door, but he grabbed her wrist and brought her along with him. "I'm going to borrow your daughter for a few minutes," he said over his shoulder.

"Be our guest," Kieran answered a bit too quickly, gaining him a mini death glare from Anne. He smiled and winked at her, as if he knew better than she what was good for her.

Jack steered her outside and toward his car. Instead of getting in, he opened the back door on the sedan, and pulled out some Rollerblades. "Put those on," he said, handing her a pair.

"It's dark out." As soon as she said it, she remembered their old routine. Sure enough, Jack produced a flashlight for each of them.

"A little night rollerblading should help work out some of your kinks." They used to skate in the dark after track meets when they'd lost, which was often enough.

Anne sat at the curb and laced up her skates, which felt a size too big, but would do. Jack did the same. In one smooth roll, he was at her side, sticking his flashlight in his back pocket, and pulling her to her feet. His strong hands were warm and did funny things to her palms. Once she'd gotten her balance, he let go and started up the street to the top of the natural slope. Anne switched on her flashlight and dug into the pavement in order to catch up. Soon they were side by side on a long and steady roll down the hill. With the nighttime breeze on her face, a full moon overhead and columns of artificial light leading the way, she recalled the excitement she used to feel skating with Jack in the dark. And Anne couldn't deny how good it felt to let go. She held out her arms and smiled into the night.

When they reached the end, she grinned at Jack. "That was great, but there's just one problem, now we have to skate back up."

He took her hand. "Come on," he said, as he pulled her along the street to the top. "Want to go again?"

She did, but all that hand holding with Jack had mixed her up and that darn nursing degree nudged its way back into her mind. "I probably shouldn't leave Mom in charge of Dad too long. Who knows what he'll talk her into next."

"You've got a point. My back still aches a little. Don't want to have to do any more rescuing tonight."

"You rescued me."

"Ah, but this was fun."

After Anne unlaced her skates, she handed them back to Jack.

"You keep them," he said. "Something tells me you may need them again."

Friday afternoon, Beverly's room mothers delivered a fifteen-foot-long get well banner made by her fourth grade class. She burst into tears on the spot and Kieran and Anne spent the rest of the evening consoling her while reading the students' wishes, after which Beverly told a cute story or anecdote about each child. With both parents giving instructions—higher, no, lower on the left, the center is drooping—Anne taped the enormous card to a family room wall. Much later that night, by the time she'd plopped into Lark's childhood bed—since Anne's old room had been redone and made into an office—in the untouched pink room with unicorn chair rail borders, she'd nearly passed out from exhaustion. Just before falling asleep, she smiled recalling her glide through the dark with Jack the night before, and later how he'd rubbed her arm when he'd said goodnight, setting off a full body tingle.

He still had the magic. Damn it.

Anne stared at the big green hill across the meadow while the coffee perked, enjoying the sway of the ash trees over the chain-link fence, thinking how peaceful her mother's little corner of the world was.

Startled by a tap, she tied her robe and walked around the counter to the sliding glass doors in the family room, and let Jocelyn in.

"You're up bright and early," Anne said, figuring Jocelyn must have come through the backyard gate adjoining their lots.

"I'm here to give you a day off."

"You don't have to do that."

"I want to."

"Don't you have a track meet or something?"

"Not this weekend."

"It's awfully sweet of you, but I'm doing fine."

Jocelyn looked at her with an expression that clearly

communicated she didn't believe a single word Anne said. She toed the tile and played with her ponytail. "Actually, I have strict orders not to take 'no' for an answer."

In need of morning coffee, Anne slanted Jocelyn a confused gaze. What were her parents up to now?

"Why don't you go get dressed?" Jocelyn said.

"Why?"

"Jack and I talked in the teacher's lounge yesterday, and he really wants to take you on a hot air balloon ride today, and—" Jocelyn glanced at her watch. "—he'll be here in twenty minutes."

## Chapter Four

Suspended in the sky beneath a blimp-sized rainbow-colored balloon, Anne gripped the thick wicker and concentrated on looking out, not down. Lush farmland divided into neat squares, patches of orchards and rows of newly developed vineyards passed in the distance. Once again, she'd forgotten the humble beauty of her hometown. Oregon was so much greener, but the yellow and brown hills of Whispering Oaks held their own special charm, and the farmland, well, it was the salt of the earth. She'd always respected the farmers who'd chosen the tougher path and held on to their land instead of selling it for tract housing developments, and her mother loved shopping at their roadside stands.

Jack skillfully fired up the propane burners whenever needed, and by ascending or descending into the air flow, he controlled their direction. His summer of apprenticeship had paid off as he piloted their balloon as if second nature.

"This is so fantastic," Anne said.

"It's relaxing, isn't it? Just what you need."

"Our nighttime skate was great, but this…"

"Yeah, nothing quite like it."

"It's the same feeling I get when I float in water." She opened her arms, taking in the entire valley vista. "Except the view is much better from here."

They smiled at each other, their gazes met and held. A spark in Jack's eyes communicated he was happy to be here with her. Heck, he'd gone out of his way to make this happen and she was flattered. She'd been aware of a small adrenaline pop in her chest when he'd picked her up earlier, and ever since something hummed nonstop through her veins. He'd brought fresh pastry and more coffee, and she'd loved the warm raspberry jam in the Danish on the drive over to Marshfield. He'd thought of everything. Like the hot air balloon, Anne decided to go with the flow for the next hour as they drifted like a behemoth birthday ball across the Whispering Oaks horizon.

After several more minutes, and additional firing of the burners, Jack stood beside her, his body heat making her edgy.

"Do you remember the first day you ever spoke to me?" he asked.

"Of course."

He looked over the valley rather than at her. "I thought you were cute," he said.

"Get out, Jack. You didn't know I existed."

"So you know better than I do?"

"Maybe."

She hoped he'd say more, but he'd evidently decided to let the conversation drop. Her mind flipped back to that first day in tenth grade, wearing her track uniform, knobby knees and all. She cringed and said out loud what she'd only meant to think. "I was such a dork."

He quirked a brow. "Offbeat maybe, but never a dork," he said, heating the balloon air, increasing their altitude and, as a result, shifting their direction back toward Marshfield.

"Yes I was. A complete dork." Who happened to be friends with one of the most popular girls in high school.

He rolled his eyes. "Here, I've got proof otherwise." He pulled out his wallet and fished for something, then produced a tattered photograph and handed it to her. It had been at least a decade since she'd seen the pose.

Brianna, Jack and Anne stood shoulder to shoulder in prom clothes, Anne's dress a conservative peach taffeta number and Brianna's a sleek silver blue. Anne remembered her father calling Brianna's a va-va-voom dress and hers, Cinderella gone country. Anne grinned studying the picture. Jack wore a traditional black tux and bow tie with a cummerbund matched perfectly to Bri's dress.

All three of them bald and grinning like asylum escapees.

"Aside from your skinhead, you looked pretty hot," he said.

The first wave of chills prickled her skin. The second made her hands shake and unlocked her tears. She handed the picture back, barely able to keep her emotions together. He put it in his shirt pocket.

Tough memories rolled over Anne in a hot gust. They'd all agreed to meet up at Anne's house for group pictures. Bri's mom and Jack's dad had arrived early, and they gathered with her parents talking in the living room, cameras and videos on the ready. Anne had spent a hundred dollars that afternoon having her hair done the way she'd always dreamed, a mass of curls and spirals cascading from the top of her head with several carefully placed rhinestone-tipped bobby pins. Brianna fretted about how badly her wig fit and how ugly it was. She'd taken it off and thrown it across the room just as Jack had arrived with the limo and rung the doorbell. Making a quick study of the situation, Jack excused himself and headed to the bathroom soon reappearing as bald as Brianna's chemo head. Never more inspired in her life, Anne marched down the hall and, as Lark looked on in horror, used her father's electric razor to shave her head, too.

She'd never done anything so daring nor had she ever been as proud in her life, even though later when her date arrived, he was mortified and embarrassed about it. Too bad, he wasn't the one she loved anyway.

Though Jack had come through for Brianna on many different occasions, that particular one had been the first night he'd locked his spot as prince of the world in Anne's heart. A prince she could never have.

Warm from the inside out, Anne looked at Jack, misty-eyed with half his mouth hitched into a smile. An ancient tomb of sadness opened between them as if a sinkhole. They slid to its center and crashed together in an embrace. The sudden move made the balloon basket rock and creak, but she ignored it, crumpling against his chest. A foreign sensation of needles pricked behind her lids and soon got replaced by tears. Jack hugged her tight and they stayed that way, sharing warmth and memories for what seemed like minutes.

The perennial valley wind blustered over them as they held on to each other. She bit her bottom lip to still her trembling chin, and stole a quick glance at him. Her feelings were mirrored there in his expression, in that aching forlorn look, the one she remembered so well from the day they'd both found out about Brianna's cancer. Jack had proved to be true-blue during those following weeks. Neither of them ever mentioned their kiss again. She held his steady, sad-eyed gaze, and in that moment she understood why she'd fallen in love with him.

"You were such a wonderful boyfriend to Brianna," she said.

His chest stiffened against hers. "You were the best friend anyone could hope for."

But she'd betrayed Brianna by falling in love with

Jack, and he'd told Anne he had feelings for her and... the cancer shamed them both out of exploring those new feelings when reality had crashed around them. What did sweet kisses under oak trees mean when your friend was dying? And after she'd died, along with the sorrow and the mourning, things were too confusing to figure out. At least they were for Anne. Life had put an end to whatever they'd started.

She could never look at Jack without that breach of Brianna's friendship tainting her thoughts.

She had no idea how Jack felt since he'd never opened up about any of it. On the last day they'd met, he'd sat there in Denny's and let her say goodbye without so much as a blink. "Moving on doesn't always mean moving forward," he'd said, as if he was the wise one.

All Anne could think of were those last remaining feelings of betrayal, remorse and shame. It had been too much to bear, and now that she was back home, it still was and she couldn't wait to leave town.

Jack rubbed her back. "We were just kids. We didn't know how to handle things," he said, as if reading her mind.

For that moment, she forced her memory back, and it was just the two of them, Jack and Anne, in a tight embrace under the colorful balloon. She clung to his solid chest and nuzzled against his neck. His tangy sport soap scent made her want to take a deep breath of him. He snuggled her closer, hooked some hair behind her ear then kissed her cheek.

She wasn't sure if she was dizzy from the elevation and a shift in the wind, or from Jack. The kiss sent her reeling even though it was nothing more than a comforting peck on the cheek.

His warm breath fanned across her cheek to her ear and he kissed her there, releasing a wave of tingles. That was *not* a mere fond kiss. Out of reflex, she pulled back to prove it wasn't her imagination or the Whispering Oaks breeze, but that it really was Jack, and she found his lips hovering above hers. She saw the stubble from the beard he'd skipped shaving that morning, and the sexy curve of his lower lip with a tiny scar at the corner. His breathing tickled her forehead as if kitten fur and she turned into the gentleness, which lined up their lips. All he had to do was press ever so lightly against hers…and things would never be the same.

She didn't move, held her breath, waiting. Her heart slipped out of rhythm.

All those months she'd sworn something snapped between them when they were kids, a look that promised more than friendship, skin prickles on the back of her neck whenever he was around, an inadvertent touch that electrified her skin…

He was so near.

She'd assumed it had always been one-sided, and she'd treasured her friendship with Brianna too much to find out. Even though those kisses under the oak tree at school had been the most intoxicating kisses of her life.

More in focus, she remembered those subversive

looks that had passed between them. Felt the rise of hair on her arms knowing he was nearby. Hesitant to admit the truth, because it would change everything, she couldn't stop herself—he'd felt it, too. It hadn't been all in her pitiful sidekick imagination.

Jack angled his head and skimmed her lips. She ignored that hitch in her throat and nuzzled into them. As if he'd been waiting for some subtle signal and had finally detected it, he planted firmer on her mouth. The connection started a warm sensation curling over her neck and shoulders. His lips were soft and he moistened hers with his tongue. His hands anchored her neck and the soft seductive kiss transformed into something hotter. He kissed like a man starving for contact. Her eager response left no question that she longed for closeness, too.

Her mouth opened and he filled her, teasing her tongue with his. Heat flamed her cheeks and breasts as she kneaded his back, pulling him closer. Every remaining barrier broke down.

Over and over, making up for missed chances and years, they kissed. *I saw you first, Jack. You were supposed to be mine.*

He exhaled, broke free, leaned his forehead to hers and whispered, "It's been a long time coming."

She sighed, secretly thrilled he'd missed kissing her. "It was definitely worth the wait."

"I don't know about the wait, but it was pretty damn spectacular on my end," he said, grinning.

She made a breathy laugh, still floating from his kiss.

He smiled against her cheek, ran his nose along her hairline releasing another squadron of tingles marching across her shoulders and deep inside her center. He seemed ready to kiss her again, and she definitely wanted him to, but he stiffened.

"Whoa!" he said, releasing her and jumping toward the burner. They'd drifted dangerously close to the strawberry crops below.

He lit the burner full-out as she internally combusted over his lingering kiss. How in the world was she supposed to act around him now? Though great friends in their teens, they were virtually strangers now. She couldn't deny the chemistry, but she really didn't know anything about him anymore.

While he increased their altitude, she worked at composing herself, which was not an easy task after their mind-blowing lip-lock. What did this mean? So what if they were still hot for each other? She hadn't come home to get involved with Jack.

Life was complicated enough dealing with her parents and their needs, juggling her new job in Portland and waiting for Lucas to come home.

The thought of digging out and exploring her stashed-away feelings for Jack scared the wits out of her. The timing was all off. As usual. Exciting as it seemed, she'd grown up, grown cautious and hadn't she seen him with a redhead last week?

She leaned on the basket, studied the rock-laden hills across the valley and the neatly squared patches of tilled land below, and swallowed an ever-thickening lump in her throat. She'd kissed Jack, again, and it had been so much more than she'd remembered.

Once he'd successfully increased their altitude and found the crosswind heading back toward Marshfield, he partially grinned, a guilty smile if she'd read that sheepish look correctly. "Too bad I have to take a shift at the fire department tonight," he said.

She studied the thick, woven branches of the basket and thought about Jack and the mysterious redhead— the perfect on paper, but "always something missing" link. He was searching for someone, and was reaching out to her. He'd told her that his mother had died when he was twelve. His best girl had died, and shortly after that, Anne had left for college. There seemed to be a pattern of women leaving him.

But damn it, he knew where she'd gone, he could have come after her if he'd really wanted to. He never had.

Anne shivered. Could she handle it if she opened her heart and Jack decided there was *still* something missing? That even if she gave her all, it might not be enough? Was there such a thing as *the one* for him? She couldn't bear to find out.

Jack was her past. Wasn't that a place you could never go back to?

"What are you doing tomorrow night?" he asked.

She bit her lip and glanced at Jack who watched her as if trying to read her mind. He was lonely and she knew exactly how that felt, and she wasn't sure she'd be able to fill that gap. Was she what Jack was really looking for, or merely someone to pass the time with while she was in town?

She glanced down at her feet. "I promised my dad I'd watch the Angels' ball game with him."

Jack gave a wry laugh and shook his head. He was probably wondering whether she'd been in the same basket with him a few seconds ago when they'd kissed each other silly. He lifted his brows. "Whatever, speedy."

Sure it was a lame excuse, but under the mind-numbing circumstances, it was the best explanation she could come up with.

Jack drove home with his thoughts spinning in a million directions. He'd finally managed more time with Anne, set up the perfect situation for the apology, gotten her to open up and be herself, then he'd blown it by planting a kiss on her that still had his socks smoking. He was supposed to apologize for the mess he'd gotten them both into all those years ago, that was the plan, but instead she'd taken a look at the picture and rushed into his arms, and he'd kissed her. What in the hell was the matter with him? She was more skittish than a kitten on catnip, and she needed time to reestablish trust in him, not a guy ravishing her in a balloon a thousand feet in the air.

He turned onto a new section of freeway and pushed on the gas.

He'd finally taken the advice from Drew; apologize to her so you can move on. He'd carried the self-inflicted guilt around his neck for thirteen years, and he really did need to man up, name it, apologize for it, release it and move forward with his life. The problem was his neatly thought-out plan had backfired.

Jack kicked up the speed another ten miles.

He'd shown Anne the picture he'd carried since high school and the memories came rushing back sweeping them both away on a crosswind of emotion. He'd taken advantage of the moment, let desire not logic win out, and he'd kissed her.

Jack sucked in a breath. Fact was he wouldn't have missed that kiss for anything in the world.

But that was definitely *not* part of the apology plan.

His smile ended when he realized he still hadn't said the words—*forgive me. I'm sorry for hurting you.*

…And he'd missed his freeway exit. Damn it all.

Thinking back, he'd been a total jerk when she'd left Whispering Oaks. He'd needed months to sort through the tightly twined ball of emotions that Brianna's illness and death had left him with. But there was Anne, sitting across from him at Denny's two months later, avoiding his eyes, her voice cracking when she strained the words, *I'm leaving for college tomorrow.*

Didn't Anne know how much he had needed her then? They'd been through hell and back together. How could she walk out at a time like that?

He'd acted like he didn't even care about her leaving, considering it emotional survival at the time. "Never let them see you care" had been his motto ever since his mother had left.

And hadn't it all started with his mother? *A boy this age only needs his father. I'm done,* she'd said, packed and ready to leave. As an adult, words couldn't begin to describe the idiocy of that statement, but as a kid…

Rather than feed the pain when his mother left, he'd put on his jock armor and told people she'd died, and from that day forward, he'd faced life with a swagger and bravado.

Anne had seen through his façade from day one, and she'd liked him anyway. He exited the freeway and doubled back on WO Boulevard. He passed the signature palm-tree-lined median balanced against the clear blue sky like a Southern California postcard, and headed for home.

Like any boy of twelve, he couldn't understand the problem was between his mother and father, not with him. But he'd taken responsibility for his mother's leaving anyway, and decided he was the reason she'd left. When she'd shown little interest in keeping in touch with him for the next few years while she traveled the country rediscovering herself, he'd had his proof. They'd reunited since he was an adult, but he couldn't trust her, and their relationship was strained. He couldn't honestly say he loved his mother the way most sons did.

What was wrong with him? Every woman he'd dated in the last decade had the same complaint, *you're too distant…I feel like you're holding back from me.*

What about that unidentifiable *something* that always seemed to be missing for him? If he could just find that old camaraderie and trust with a woman that he'd once had with Anne, maybe things could be different.

Jack took a winding road leading up to his street. A few towering pine trees graced the path that heralded his turnoff.

Now that she was home, he had the perfect opportunity to make amends and maybe, just maybe, once he did, he'd finally be ready to find a woman he could love.

Back on task, the apology was top of his list.

Jack pulled into the driveway for his townhome and parked—grateful he had the distraction of a shift at the fire department that night. He'd said the words a million times in his head, but so far he couldn't get his lips to move when around Anne. They'd hiked, and skated, and ballooned together, yet he still hadn't told her that he was sorry. God, he was sorry. Determined not to miss the opportunity since she wouldn't be in town for long, he fished for his cell phone, and punched in a familiar number.

"Hey, Kieran, I hear the Angels are playing tomorrow night. Feel like some guy company?"

He grinned a subversive grin while Kieran played right into his plan.

"Sweet! What time should I be there?"

"I'll get it!" Beverly said when the doorbell rang at 7:00 p.m. Bart trotted after her with an enthusiastic *woof!*

Anne listened to the quickening snaps of microwave

popcorn, enjoying the buttery smell, and let her mother get the door. She focused on the job at hand, willing to do anything to erase the kiss of a lifetime from yesterday. So far, even though she'd been running all day with grocery shopping, laundry and preparing meals, she'd been completely unsuccessful at forgetting it.

Why was it that the top three kisses of her life had all been from Jack?

And when had any guy ever come close to matching the wildfire effect of one of those kisses? Even while trying *not* to think about the kiss, while secretly savoring and reliving every second of it, her cheeks warmed and her lips still tingled twenty-four hours later.

Man oh man, Jack knew how to light her fire.

"Hey, Jack!" Her father's baritone voice snapped her out of her hot haze.

What? After dinner she'd showered and slipped on her threadbare gray sweatpants, and one of her brother's old extra-large T-shirts, sans bra. Scrubbed clean, she'd left out her contact lenses reverting to her clunky rectangular black-framed glasses, and she'd swept up her hair into a knot that left half of it dangling in clumps on her neck.

What was he doing here, and more importantly, how could she face him looking like this?

The daydreamy kiss-charged warmth had now fanned into a full blown blush of embarrassment. With her flaming cheeks, she probably looked like she'd just run the hundred-meter dash.

Cursing the remodeled open and flowing kitchen

and family room, she looked for a method of escape. She could slip out the back door and zip from bush to bush to the sliders in her parents' bedroom and let herself in there. Or, she could wiggle her nose and desperately hope to disappear. Since he was already inside the house, and she'd never mastered magic, she'd have to settle for glaring at the microwave.

"Hi."

She jerked her head around. There he was. Tight jeans. Formfitting, button-up shirt. A quirky smile on his face.

"H...hi."

"I'm on beer duty," he said, as naturally as if he lived there, while walking toward the refrigerator with Bart hot on his heels. "Want some help with that?" He nodded toward the microwave.

She'd lost track of the popcorn, and the distinct scent of burnt kernels drew her out of her panic. Bart sniffed the air. She stopped the microwave, opened the door and let a tendril of smoke curl out. Folding her arms high across her chest, she rushed across the kitchen. "I think I hear my cell phone. I'll cook another bag in a minute."

Fifteen minutes later, and well into the first inning of the ball game, Anne slipped back into the room and sat on the opposite end of the couch Jack inhabited. Her parents both cast her quizzical glances, Mom putting more suspicion into hers. She'd changed into jeans and two-tone double layered tank tops, this time wearing her bra, a push-up bra, and enough makeup not to be obvious.

Jack had cooked more popcorn and passed the large bowl her way.

"It's one to nothing, the Rangers," he said, glancing sideways, but making a quick assessment of her change of clothes.

She took a handful of popcorn and shoved half of it into her mouth with Bart eagerly watching for any fall-out. Her father booed the TV when a player got another hit off the Angels' pitcher.

"Annie, will you refill my lemonade?" her mother asked. She'd gotten used to being waited on and some-times resorted to taking advantage. Her arm might be in a cast, but she had complete use of her legs, and Anne had been meaning to mention that fact to her.

Except this time, Anne was grateful for the excuse to get away from Jack, so she grabbed her mother's glass and headed back to the kitchen.

If Jack thought he could insinuate himself into her life, he had another thing coming. She was over him. So over him. She had a new life and job and she lived over nine hundred miles away. But as she poured herself a glass along with her mother's lemonade, she shook her head and pinched her lips together rather than smile. She had to admit, the situation with Jack pretending he was part of the family was amusing.

"The bums," her father groused over another messed up play.

Anne returned with the lemonade and sat by her

mother. Jack recited a baseball player's recent stats, and Kieran listened as if Jack had the solution for world peace. Beverly smiled, mindlessly rubbing Bart's ear and obviously content to be at home with her husband and his guest on a Sunday night. The picture felt a little too Norman Rockwell for Anne's taste, but who was she to complain? She was just as much a visitor in her parents' home as Jack was and, if having him around made her parents happy, well, she'd have to live with that…as long as she was here.

Midsip, Anne made a snap decision to quit letting Jack make her so uptight. He used to be the person she looked forward to seeing at school the most. And regardless how slow she was on the track field, he'd always cheered her on until she'd crossed the finish line, then acted as if she was in first place. He was the guy who got all of her corny jokes, and vice versa. And, he was a *Star Trek* nerd, too. They used to practice the Spock hand gesture until the splayed finger wave came natural. Of course, Jack would only do it when none of his jock friends were around, but he'd done it enough to let Anne know they'd had something special between them. It had been their secret code.

Anne downed half of her lemonade and fought off the intense desire to pucker.

So why had Jack fallen for her best friend? Maybe he was just a typical high school guy, full of himself, seeing how much he could get away with. Maybe that was why he'd kissed her way back then. But he didn't have to say those words…

All these years later, back in her hometown, there was only one major difference—she wasn't in high school anymore. She was a big girl who could handle anything life threw at her. Hadn't she already proved that?

But what about yesterday? So what if she'd rushed into his arms, he sure as hell didn't have to kiss her. She glanced up midthought, connecting with Jack's gaze from across the family room. He discreetly lifted his hand and made the Spock gesture.

Anne's shoulders slumped as she dutifully flashed the split finger wave, shook her head, and took another swig of lemonade as if it were a shot of whisky.

Monday afternoon, Anne set her mother's hair while she sat at the kitchen table with her neon pink cast propped on a pillow. Threads of afternoon sun spun through the windows and across the light oak floor. The leftover aroma of bacon from breakfast still hung in the air.

"Since when have you and Dad gotten so buddy-buddy with Jack?"

Her mother handed her another curler. "When Jack started working at the high school, and before Jocelyn transferred over, he signed on to help with the hurdlers." Beverly clucked her tongue. "I think your dad has really missed having Lucas around, and Jack kind of helped fill the void."

Anne's brows shot up. Dad and Lucas had done nothing but fight the last few years before Anne had gone away to college. She distinctly remembered hearing her father tell her mother that Lucas showed all the signs of being a slacker. Is that the same kid her dad missed?

Slacker wasn't at all how Anne had seen her brother. Lucas worked nonstop rebuilding the engine on his classic '64 Mustang he'd badgered Dad into letting him buy with his own hard-earned money from mowing lawns and delivering papers, long before he was old enough to drive it. He'd always shown passion for whatever he loved, like reading fantasy books and playing video war games. The problem was, he didn't love school, and as soon as he had graduated, he shocked everyone by heading off for army boot camp instead of enrolling in trade school like they'd discussed.

Dad had been majorly disappointed but kept silent on the subject of his son who'd turned his back on education, the backbone of both his parents' lives.

"Jack has a lot going for him, wouldn't you say?" Beverly said, obviously prodding a response.

Anne snapped out of pondering over her brother, and decided to be noncommittal about Jack as she rolled the next section of hair. "He's always been a great guy, Mom. He'll make some woman happy someday."

"Speaking of making someone happy, have you got any new beaus?"

Stopping midcurl, she grimaced. Damn, she'd opened the door for the dreaded conversation.

She'd spare her mother the news of her not having a serious date in close to a year. It would only upset her. "I've been kind of busy with the new job and all. There are a couple single doctors in the practice, though. One isn't too bad, but the other thinks he's the prince of Persia."

"Don't your friends ever fix you up?"

Fix her up? How humiliating. Her sad dating situation hadn't come to that point yet, had it? What about that med student she'd liked for a little while. Sure, it was sort of embarrassing that he was four years her junior, but still, there was something about him that made her sit up and take notice. It wasn't like she wasn't trying completely.

"Well, I did go to a costume party last Halloween with a guy in med school."

Maybe she could divert the topic away from Jack if she gave her mother proof she went on dates. "Here, let me show you." She found her purse on the kitchen counter and opened her wallet, hoping her mother wouldn't calculate how long ago that date actually was, then brandished their picture. He'd gone as Austin Powers and she was Felicity Shagwell. "Here it is." She passed the picture to her mother, wondering why she even kept the dang thing. Maybe because she liked her silly costume and thought she looked kind of hot. Hot for Anne Grady, anyway.

Beverly blurted out a laugh, "This is cute," then squinted and stared, "Hmm. Hand me my glasses, would you please?"

Anne trotted around the table to the granite counter where the glasses lay. "Here you go."

Beverly slipped them on and scrutinized the photo as if studying a legal document. "He looks like Jack."

"He...what?" Anne snatched back the picture and glanced at it then looked closer. Her date wore Austin Powers glasses and silly gold medallions around his neck. "He does not."

"Of course he does. He's Jack ten years ago."

Anne blinked and looked harder at the image of the dark-blond, wavy-haired guy with his Christmas card smile and crinkled, friendly eyes, green eyes to be exact, then swallowed.

No wonder she'd been attracted to him.

Anne rolled her eyes, and when her cell phone beeped the arrival of a text message, she almost said a prayer of thanksgiving. "I've got to get this, Mom. It might be Lark."

She dug back into her purse and found her phone.

Wanna watch the latest Star Trek DVD with me tonight?

It was Jack....

"Okay, five more minutes to finish the chapter test," Jack said, checking his watch. "If you've already finished, bring them up to my desk."

His cell vibrated, and he quickly checked for Anne's response.

How about Wednesday night?

Now he was getting somewhere. He grinned, thinking about their kiss for about the tenth time that day, which was not at all the reason he'd sexted…uh…texted her.

Your house or mine?

A few seconds later his cell vibrated again… mine?

Okay, she was playing it safe, but maybe Beverly and Kieran would give them some time alone and he could apologize.

Sounds good. C U then.

Glancing at the clock with five more minutes until the end of sixth period, and with another flashback to a great kiss, he mindlessly fiddled with his cell phone keyboard.

Anne + Jack = KABOOM!

He was just horsing around killing time, had no intention of sending the message.

"We're not supposed to use cell phones in class, Mr. Lightfoot," a short dark-haired student said, handing in his math test.

Surprised, Jack tossed the cell into his desk drawer, hitting *end* as he did. "You're right, Manish. Rules must apply to everyone. I apologize."

The scrawny teen nodded and pushed his overbearing glasses up his long nose.

After he accepted the test sheet, Jack opened his desk drawer and got hit with an awkward surprise—*message sent* his cell reported.

He pushed away his chair, rubbed the back of his neck and glanced at the ceiling, all the while hustling for an excuse. How in the hell was he supposed to explain the slipup? Deep in thought, his cell vibrated, and disregarding school rules and Manish's admonishment, he opened the drawer and checked the response…which put an amused smile on his face.

Kaboom back at ya. :)

Well hot damn, what was he supposed to make of that?

## Chapter Five

The phone rang. Kieran moved as fast as his crutches would cooperate to answer it. In the middle of brushing out her mother's hair, Anne let him. He'd gotten more confident with the crutches over the last few days, while his boredom had soared.

"Lucas!" The smile on her father's face stretched broadly, and Anne had to admit, he had a great smile. "How ya been, son?"

At the sound of Lucas's name, Beverly sat straighter, attention, like a guided missile, heading straight to the phone.

Insisting on being in the middle of things, Bart paced back and forth between Kieran and Beverly.

"No kidding. This Friday? That's great news!"

Anne and her mother grinned at each other like kids hearing Santa slide down the chimney.

"What time?" Beverly called out. Bart lifted his ears and tilted his head.

Kieran swatted the air and gave her an I'm-not-an-idiot glare. "What time is your plane due in?"

"Tell him that I'll pick him up," Anne called out, receiving a double air swipe and an impatient squint.

"Annie belle will be there. Can't wait to see you, son."

While Kieran scribbled down the info, Anne and her mom high-fived, and Anne noticed Beverly used her casted arm. She was getting pretty comfortable hoisting that thing, maybe soon she could start doing more for herself. Maybe even go back to teaching school with the help of a teacher's aide. A girl could hope, couldn't she?

"You're going to help me bake his favorite cake on Friday, okay?" Beverly said.

"Of course, Mom."

With Kieran's spirits obviously lifted—a welcomed sight since lying around the house had seemed to make her dad lethargic and testy the last couple days—he put a little more jaunt in his single-foot step, swinging on the crutches down the hall like a man on a mission. Bart, of course, was hot on his trail.

Anne and Beverly went back to making plans for Lucas's homecoming and debating whether to call Lark or not. She'd wanted to come home, and knowing the whole family would be here might only make her hankering worse, but regardless, she deserved to know.

"You should call her," Anne said, putting the final coat of spray on Beverly's layered and casual hairdo. With all the practice she'd been getting styling her mother's hair, she could open her own shop for stylish seniors.

Anne checked the clock and hoped they wouldn't interrupt any of Lark's classes, as her mother speed dialed Boston.

"Hi, Larky!" her mom soon sang.

*Larky-malarkey* Anne used to tease her little sister who seemed to get everything she ever wanted.

Beverly filled in her daughter on the latest news then listened for a long time. It sounded like Lark had a lot to tell her.

"You haven't been feeling well? How long has this been going on?"

"Is she eating?" Anne asked, old worries rushing like a stampede through her mind.

Lark had fooled everyone for months when she'd been in high school, until her parents had let her fly up to Oregon to visit Anne for a weekend. Alarmed by her appearance—instead of fashionably thin, she'd looked gaunt and unhealthy—Anne had kept an eye on her sister. She'd picked at her food, moving things around instead of actually eating, and later at the movies, Anne had put her arm around her sister's waist. Lark's bony hips felt more like a preteen, and it had unnerved her.

Then, she'd run her hand up Lark's razor-sharp spine. When had she gotten so skinny?

Lark had always been the perfect one—the perfect daughter, the perfect student. That night, Anne had finally realized that Lark had also become the perfect anorexic, hiding her disease from her family…until then. She'd broken into tears and hugged her little sister.

*"We'll get you through this, Larky-malarkey. I promise." Anne hugged her again, and felt the bundle of knobs and bones that had become the sum of her sister's scrawny body. She held Lark tightly, and as the moments passed, felt her relax.*

After a family intervention, pure determination on Lark's part during her treatment, coupled with the complete support of her family, had worked wonders on her recovery. She'd been fit and healthy for eight years. Now, with Lark so far away, with a stressful schedule in med school, knowing there was no such thing as a perfect med student, Anne prayed things hadn't backtracked. They hadn't seen each other in over a year, and Anne was curious how she looked.

Beverly covered the phone. "She say's she feels nauseated a lot of the time, but wants to eat everything in sight the rest of the time. She said to tell you not to worry—she hasn't lost a single pound."

Anne let go a sigh of relief, just as a huge crash came from down the hall. On impulse, she charged toward the sound coming from her brother's old bedroom. She flung herself through the opened door as if breaking a tape at the finish line, and found her father on his side with Bart licking his face.

"Are you okay?" she said, winded.

"The damn blasted box was heavier than I thought." He glanced up, a grimace on his face.

On her way down to her knees, Anne glanced into the opened closet, and the empty space on the top shelf where her father must have tried to remove the box. But how?

"What happened?" Beverly arrived on scene, her left hand cupping her mouth. She dropped to her knees on Kieran's other side. "Honey, are you okay?"

He winced and ducked his head. "I can't move my arm."

Anne knew a fractured arm when she saw one, and shook her head wondering how much more could go wrong.

"Mom, stay with him. I'll call 9–1–1 and get something to splint your arm, Dad."

Fifteen minutes later, a shrill siren whooped out front. She'd propped her father up at the bedside and splinted his forearm with rolled up newspapers and duct tape, then placed a plastic bag filled with ice over the quickly swelling wrist area. She'd also put his casted leg on a couple pillows to prevent any swelling in his foot.

The doorbell rang and she bolted down the hall and opened the door. "He's right in here." Anne let the two emergency techs into the house and led them to her brother's room. Their work boots reverberated down the hardwood hall behind her.

The serious-eyed tech went right to work checking up on Kieran. His female partner, wearing a girlish ponytail that offset the unflattering uniform, took the history.

"He was in a motorcycle accident a couple weeks ago, and he lost his balance and fell in here. No one was with him."

The young woman's eyebrows shot up in understanding.

"He didn't ask for help," Anne clarified, slanting a frustrated look her father's way.

Mom hovered over Dad, fidgeting with his hair, and smoothing his shirt over and over. When Anne's cell phone rang, seeing it was Lark, she passed it to her mother for distraction.

Beverly went into her version of what happened, and Anne didn't bother to correct a few minor details: Her father had used one crutch to edge a storage box off a high closet shelf. What had he been thinking? Evidently the box came tumbling down and he lost his balance using his hand to break the fall and with the heavy box landing on top of his forearm.

"I thought it would be nice to put out some of Lucas's track trophies and medals, is all," he said.

The gesture touched Anne's heart—at least her father and brother had one thing in common, a love for track—but she was still annoyed at him for doing something so stupid and for being so damn independent he couldn't ask for help.

As both EMTs performed a quick assessment on her father, another siren grew closer, soon rounding the corner of the cul de sac. Anne barely noticed it, preoccupied with her father's care.

"Hey, speedy, what happened?" Jack's voice offered immediate comfort.

"Oh, Jack, I'm so glad you're here." Really? Since when?

He rubbed her shoulder. "Broken arm?"

She nodded, overwhelmed and on the verge of tears. She couldn't stand seeing her father, the big strong mainstay of the household, on the ground, helpless and in pain.

Jack gave her a single-armed hug. "Kieran, I thought I warned you about crossing Anne."

Grateful he'd tried to lighten the mood, she cuffed his shoulder and gave a halfhearted laugh, as they rolled her father out of the bedroom on a gurney.

"Nah," Kieran said, sounding resigned, "I won this prize all by myself."

Anne and Beverly sat in the E.R. waiting room. She stared at the bland linoleum as her father got transported to radiology for an official X-ray. She'd been spending far too much time in the place since her return home. The yammering TV and constant chill from the hyperactive automatic E.R. doors, plus an odd mix of restlessness and fatigue, made it hard to sit still. Her mother kept sighing, with tears leaking from the corners of her eyes.

"Everything's going to be okay," Anne said, patting her arm.

She glanced down the hall and noticed a coffee machine. Boy, she had to be desperate to drink that stuff, but how bad could a cup of sweetened black tea be? "Want some coffee, Mom?"

Beverly shook her head and sighed for the umpteenth time in the last ten minutes.

Anne wandered down the hall and dropped in her coins then pressed E3. Down plopped the paper cup and steaming brown brew.

She'd surreptitiously watched Jack back at her house with an ever-tightening fist in the vicinity of her sternum. He fit in with the firemen as if he'd been on the job for a decade. As she blew over the cup, that fist clutched her chest again. It bothered her that he was on her mind so much lately.

After a cautious sip, she opted to stand in the lobby rather than go back to the detention-hall feel of the waiting room. She waved her mother over as she noticed a gurney rolling toward the back entry to the E.R.

"Looks like Dad is back, let's go."

In the bustling E.R. main room, a burly resident flipped the X-rays on the view box and clucked his tongue as Anne and her mother rushed to Kieran's side. Someone Anne used to go to high school with worked as an RN here and gave a wave. Anne waved back, grateful for a friendly face.

The nurse approached. "How've you been?"

They exchanged small talk, quickly catching up. Anne pointed to her father, whom the nurse remembered from high school.

"I'll try to speed things up a bit," the nurse said after a lightning quick hug.

A minute later the doctor approached their cubicle. "Well, you hit the jackpot, Mr. Grady. You broke both the radius and ulna."

Anne's breath whooshed from her lungs. She knew what the "jackpot" meant.

"We'll need to do surgery, put in a plate and screws, before we can cast you," he said.

Beverly's forehead became a pyramid of lines. "Another surgery? Oh, no." Her good hand shot to her brow as tears dripped down her cheeks.

Kieran reached for her arm and squeezed. "Look at the bright side, babe, unlike you, I'm left-handed," he said in a noble attempt to lessen the blow.

That got an anemic chuckle out of her, but her tears were far from drying up. Anne bit back her feelings, knowing she needed to stay strong for her family. All she had to do was hold tight until Lucas got home. Having his help would mean the world to all of them.

Unaware of the small drama playing out between the Gradys, the E.R. resident cleared his voice. "I'll send my nurse in with the consent." And, as if his small contribution to the care of his latest patient was finished, he left without a syllable of encouragement.

With nerves grated right down to the bone, Anne grit

her teeth and explained how the surgery would work before the consent-wielding nurse, her friend from high school, had a chance to approach the gurney. With no other choice, Kieran signed it. Good thing he was left-handed.

Four cups of tea and as many hours later, eyes grainy from lack of sleep, Anne stretched out her legs in the surgery waiting room chair with the permanently sunken butt cushion, resting her head against the wall and watched her mother lightly snore.

"Thought I might find you here," Jack said.

She'd blame the jolt and explosion of nerves in her stomach on being caught in the near doze-zone. "It's two a.m.," she said. "What are you doing here?"

"Just rolled on another call that wound up in the ER. Got an update on your dad, so I thought I'd check things out."

"That's sweet of you, Jack, but don't you have to teach tomorrow?"

"Yep. Just like every sleepless Wednesday," he whispered since Beverly was dozing.

"Sleepless..."

"That's what my students call it." Jack sat next to Anne and took her hand. "They look forward to Wednesdays." He looked into her face and seeing her obvious concern, squeezed her fingers. "Your being here is a whole lot of comfort for your parents. Nothing can take the place of family."

Anne nodded, as a chill went through her, realizing how Jack had missed out in that regard. In high school, he'd given the impression of never needing anything or anyone, but she'd seen through his jock facade. When she'd found out, through Brianna, that Jack's mother had died when he was twelve, it had made her cry. Right then, she'd promised to always be there for him. And she had been. When Brianna had died, she didn't let him go through it alone. She'd sat by his side, not saying a word, just wanting him to know someone cared. She had understood she could never take Brianna's place, she knew she was nothing compared to her, and that Jack's kiss had been nothing more than a whim, especially since he'd never mentioned it again.

All she had wanted to do was help make his grief a little easier, because that was what friends were for.

Truth was she had needed him as much as she thought he had needed her. Did he ever understand that? But he'd pushed her away. He'd closed up as if he believed she alone had betrayed her friend and he'd had nothing to do with it.

"Didn't you used to want to be a doctor?" he asked.

"That's what I had dreamed about doing when I had no clue how much it cost."

"I thought you'd be great at it. You always cut right to the heart of any issue, you had fantastic powers of deduction and you loved all those science classes. I would have failed chemistry if you hadn't been my lab partner."

She laughed, remembering how he'd depended on her to explain the lab experiments, and more importantly to show him how to analyze and log the results.

"Hey, that's what friends are for. But seriously, I'm just as happy being a nurse."

"Remember when Bri and I drove you to the SATs?"

"You almost made me late!"

"Yeah, well, we got you there on time, and we came back later and picked you up, too."

"I was so exhausted."

"And I bought you a hot fudge sundae."

She nodded, almost able to taste it. "And I cried the whole time I ate it because I was positive I'd failed everything."

"But you did great."

"Good enough to get into the university of my choice."

"More than good enough."

She sighed. "As it turned out, yes…but it didn't matter."

He cupped her arm. "It did matter, Anne. You nailed it."

He'd always been a big supporter, and she tried to return the consideration. "I think you believed in me more than I believed in myself back then."

"Someone had to."

He'd always been a good friend, then he'd kissed her and mixed her up and went back to being just a friend. She'd wanted so much more, but had to settle for so much less.

"In fact, a little birdie told me that in college you took the MCATs and could have applied to med school, too."

On a whim, before totally giving up her dream, she'd taken the medical school entry exams her third year in college, hoping she might change her parents' minds if she'd scored well. How had he found out about that?

"Didn't matter. By then I was set on being a nurse. I just did it to see how I'd score."

Anne sipped her tea and glanced at Jack, remembering how after they'd graduated from high school, for a couple months they'd hang out, just to check up on each other. By then, it was apparent that no sparks flew from his side of the coffee shop table. Whatever magic they'd created had died along with Brianna, but Anne would never forget that once he'd kissed her and he'd passed her a note saying, "You're the one." She'd seen it with her own eyes. It hadn't been her imagination, even if she'd only fallen for an insensitive, adolescent, how-many-girls-can-I-get-to-fall-in-love-with-me game.

And right now, he was here with his hand on her arm, attempting to offer support.

"I really appreciate you stopping by, but shouldn't you be getting back to work?" she whispered, through a croak in her throat.

He patted her hand. "Right, I gotta run. Listen, let me know when he gets discharged, and I'll bring him home, again."

She gave a grateful nod, unsure if she wanted to depend on Jack so much. "I'm sure the hospital can arrange for transportation."

"I'm available if you need me. Hey, don't suppose we'll be watching *Star Trek* tomorrow night now."

"Can I take a rain check?"

"Name the day, speedy, and I'll be there."

# Chapter Six

"See that, they're letting me go home for good behavior," Kieran said the next afternoon as the nurse left the hospital room. His light brown hair stuck up in several directions giving him a trendy grandpa kind of look.

"That's great, Dad. Now all I have to do is figure out how to get you there." She really didn't want to become too dependent on Jack.

His eyes looked a bit glazed, and Anne figured the mild pain medicine might have something to do with the model patient demeanor. She smiled at her dad who'd been through so much in the past two weeks. He winked, his usual crystal blue eyes dulled by the second surgery in as many weeks, and her heart squeezed seeing him so far off his game.

"You know the man with the van," he said with a goofy half smile.

Oh, Lord, he'd started rhyming, the silly thing he'd slip into whenever he got tipsy at Christmas or New Year's, right before he put on Hall & Oates classics and started dancing with Mom. The meds must have completely kicked in.

"You mean Jack? Why can't the hospital arrange for transportation?"

"My health insurance doesn't cover that, so it would cost a fortune, and as you know, I've got a daughter in med school, and Jack already knows how to get me into that van, and…"

She sighed. "Okay, I get it. I'll call him."

As long as she was in Whispering Oaks, Jack would be infused into her life. Truth was, she needed him until Lucas got home. The trick would be not letting her guard down and falling for him again. She'd already slipped up by kissing him, not to mention sending that stupid reply to his email, but what the heck was he doing texting her such an obvious message? Anne + Jack = Kaboom!

Another sigh escaped her lips as she dug through her purse for her phone. Some things could never be repeated in life, and Jackson Lightfoot was definitely one of them. Friends forever, dude. Lovers never.

She shook her head and speed dialed Jack's cell number.

*Two more days until Lucas gets home.*

\* \* \*

"Why don't you stick around for dinner?" Kieran said, now that he was propped up on one of the family room couches, foot and opposite arm elevated, dog at his feet, gazing expectantly at his master.

Jack rubbed his back and stretched. He'd spent more time at the Gradys' house in the past two weeks then he had the entire two years in high school he'd hung out with Anne. "Sounds like a plan. Besides, someone is going to have to get you to bed later."

"Good point."

While Beverly fussed with the pillow under Kieran's arm, and Bart licked the fingers protruding from the cast, Jack glanced over his shoulder at Anne.

"Are you okay? Do you need more pain medicine?" Beverly asked.

"I'm just dandy, babe." Kieran was definitely feeling no pain.

Anne's usual bright eyes seemed a bit dull with worry. Her nutmeg-colored hair shone and rested on the shoulders of a pink plaid country-gone-urban styled blouse. Snug-fitting, straight-leg jeans reminded him that she'd grown a few curves, and look at that, a nice treat he hadn't expected—pink toenails peeked out from no less than two-inch platform flip-flops. He liked what he saw, and getting to stick around for dinner was a definite bonus.

If he was lucky, he might get a chance to explain that text message, but how could he justify Anne + Jack = Kaboom! Should he come clean and tell her that he'd never meant to send it? Then why write it? He could practically hear the incredulity in her tone, and imagined her dissecting stare as it made him feel like a total idiot. Was there a logical way out of this? Maybe he'd let it drop. Pretend it never happened. Coward.

"You want some cold water or iced tea or anything?" she asked, avoiding his obvious gaze.

"I'm good. Thanks." He scratched his upper lip with his thumb. "You need any help in there?"

"You've done enough already, Jack. Sit down and relax and I'll call everyone when dinner's ready."

Well, shoot, that meant he couldn't get close enough in the kitchen to smell her hair or, if he was lucky, brush against her by accident.

"I'm not doing anything fancy—do chicken tacos, rice and pinto beans sound okay for everyone?"

Okay, he had a way in. He was the master of grating cheese and chopping tomatoes, and he'd shred cabbage if she wanted, or lettuce. Her call. He'd give her a couple minutes to get started, then he'd wander in for some water or something and...

Ten minutes later, while Anne cooked the meat and added the premeasured spices, Jack filled a large glass with filtered tap water then washed his hands. He took a drink and went right to the knife block for the tomato slicer. "I brought the *Star Trek* DVD, maybe after dinner we can all watch it. Hey, pass me those tomatoes and I'll get them started for you." Was that slick enough?

Anne looked over her shoulder, hesitated, but did what he asked.

He washed the vegetables and left them at the sink when Beverly came into the kitchen and attempted to pour some lemonade for herself and Kieran. Bart followed, like there might be a treat involved.

"Let me get that, Bev," he said, stepping over to her aid.

After he'd carried the drinks out to the family room, where the TV blasted tomorrow's weather, he rushed back to his tomato task. Anne lightly browned corn tortillas on an iron griddle and placed them into a warmer, while stirring the meat in the skillet. Rice steamed on a back burner, and canned pinto beans heated on another. For someone who professed not to be a cook, she looked at ease and totally in control. The domestication suited her.

"Don't tell my mother, but I bought pre-shredded lettuce and packaged seasoning," she murmured out of the side of her mouth.

He leaned close enough to whisper into her ear, allowing him to inhale the light coconut scent of her hair. "My lips are sealed," he said, studying her smooth, long neck and wondering if she'd mind if he slipped a few kisses along the delicate curve.

She jabbed her elbow into his ribs. "You're in the way," she chided, moving the latest batch of tortillas from the griddle to the warmer.

He took one last smell of her, which was quickly getting overpowered by the spicy aroma of taco meat, and got back to tomato duty safely away at the chopping block island.

She'd definitely whetted his appetite for an after dinner make-out session. Hell, just being around her sent his mind in that direction. Too bad that they'd all be watching the latest Spock and Captain Kirk adventures instead of Anne and him making good use of that old-fashioned two-person patio swing.

"On the count of three…one…two…three!" Jack said, taking the brunt of Kieran's weight, while Anne transferred the casted leg farther onto the bed. Thump! With their help and supervisions, her father had angled himself from the wheelchair into standing on his one good leg. He'd pivoted with Jack and Anne on both sides as Beverly pulled the wheelchair away, and sat on the edge of his king-size bed just long enough to catch his breath. Jack had climbed onto the bed and bear-hugged Kieran, and Anne had taken her post beside his cast, before he counted to three.

"Did I mention how much I hate this?" Kieran said.

How in the world would they have gotten Dad to bed without his help?

"Deal with it, Dad."

Anne crumpled onto the bed, and Jack slumped against the headboard. Kieran lay flat, waiting for a pillow until Beverly rushed over with a couple and tucked them under his head. Bart sat at the bedside watching, whining as if planning how to get up on the bed, too.

"This is the most people I've ever been in bed with," Kieran said, a little out of breath, and obviously riding the high of his bedtime medication.

"TMI, Dad!" Anne playfully socked him with the pillow she was about to prop under his leg cast.

"And not true, sweetie," Beverly said, fussing with his receding hairline. "Remember how we and the kids used to crowd in here on the nights when the wind got so strong we thought it would lift off our roof?"

"Ah, yes," Kieran said. "The good old days with the Santa Anas and the munchkins."

"And after the earthquake," Anne said. "We all slept together for at least a week."

"I stand corrected. Now, will someone please scratch the bottom of my foot?"

Beverly jumped to action.

Anne glanced at Jack. He'd rolled onto his back and propped his head on the bend of his elbow, which forced a natural bulge from his deltoid, and made him look more like a male model than an old *friend*.

As if sensing her watching him, his gaze drifted to her and he gave a quick smile—there was that spark again. She looked away in a flash.

"Well, I guess I'd better be going," he said, taking his time standing. "Get a good night's sleep, Kieran, and I'll come by on my way to school in the morning to help you get back into that chair." He pointed to the wheelchair with the extra egg crate cushion.

Anne wanted to blurt out *we'll manage* but knew

there was no way she and her mother could handle the job. "Thanks, Jack."

"Yes," Beverly chimed in, "we can't thank you enough."

He smiled and nodded at her parents, then turned to her. "Walk me out?" he said, with lifted brows and hands shoved in back jean pockets.

She nodded and followed him down the hall.

"Dinner was great," he said.

"I'm glad you enjoyed it."

He opened the door, but paused.

"You've been a huge help," she said. "Thanks again."

She intended to stay at the door and watch him walk down the path to his car then wave good-night, but he grabbed her and pulled her onto the porch, then backed her up against the brick trim. A quick flash of another time and place when his fingers had grasped her wrist and tugged her behind an old oak tree came to mind.

Jack leaned toward her, hands balanced on the wall on both sides of her head. "We need to talk," he said, the porch light glinting off his pupils.

She felt the need to swallow, but her throat had gone dry. "About?"

He studied her face. "Lots of things." He blew out a breath. "So many things." He glanced at his watch. "The problem is, it's after eleven, I had about three hours sleep last night, and I need more time to explain everything, and I don't want to do anything halfway."

His nearness set her breathing out of sync.

"Our timing always sucked," he said.

Normally, she could come up with a dozen smart-aleck ideas to challenge or lighten any moment, but mesmerized by Jack in such close proximity, nothing came to mind. Distracted by his sharp shaving gel scent, and the heat of his body so close to hers, he'd thrown her off track. All she could do was watch him. She noticed the muscle at his jaw grip and relax, as if holding back a whole lot of words, and, damn it all to hell, she wanted to know what they were.

She cleared her throat fearing what their topic of conversation would be yet dying to finally get things out in the open. *That kiss was a mistake, Anne. I never should have done it.* Forcing her focus away from his intent eyes, she stared at his chin…and that tiny scar at the corner of his mouth just begging her to touch it.

Had he never wanted her at all?

"Tell me," she whispered.

He dipped his head and nipped her neck, which felt like a mini lightning hit across her skin. Then he backed away as if he'd felt it, too.

"Sunday. Come out with me Sunday."

"I may not have the chance."

"Make time." He glanced at her, eyes drifting back to her neck, then he took a step toward his car, leaving her tingling and filled with questions.

Why had she handed off total control to him, and why was he being such a tease? Her stomach muscles tensed, she fisted her hands and lunged for his arm then swung him around.

"You can't plant a kiss on my neck like that, tell me

we've got to talk, then walk away as if nothing just happened."

He pulled in his chin, his eyebrows shot up. "I wouldn't call that a kiss, speedy. That was a peck."

"Whatever you call it, Jack, quit playing games with me. I don't understand what you're doing. Or why you're doing it. Why now?"

His expression changed from amused to serious as he ducked his head and scratched his upper lip with his thumb. "Because I owe you a major apology, Anne, and it's hard to get it out. It's stuck right here in my throat, choking me every time I see you."

An apology. Maybe it was the constant evening breeze rustling through the bushes and over her skin, but his scooting-around-the-edges admission sent the whisper of a shiver over her chest and arms.

"It would mean the world to me to hear it. Any part of it." Her voice sounded quivery.

"Spend the day with me, Sunday."

"Right now, Jack. I want to hear something right now."

His hands went to his hips, he bent his head. A random rock on the steps got his total attention while he kicked it aside and shook his head. "We were young, Anne. We didn't know what the hell we were doing. I was a jerk. You probably thought I wanted it all. My buddy, speedy. Your sexy best friend." He glanced at her, then quickly down the street. "Truth was, I always liked you, but I never got the impression you wanted to be anything but friends. And I didn't want to mess with that."

He pinned his stare on her eyes. She tried not to blink, didn't want to do anything to distract or stop him. Bottom line, he sure as hell had done something to mess with their friendship. And, yeah, come to think of it, he did owe her a damn apology!

"Bri flirted with me all the time, and I thought it was okay with you if I asked her out." His eyes fused with hers. "You acted like everything was fine, so we all just kept hanging out." He shook his head. "But then I noticed something. It only worked when we were all together. Brianna was beautiful and I wanted her—" he shrugged his arms "—but something was missing when we were by ourselves."

He turned his head and glanced down the street again. Anne didn't want to breathe, afraid if she did, he'd notice and shut up. But God only knew, she needed to hear this. Maybe it would finally help her figure things out. To forgive herself…and him. She took a step forward.

"After the initial thrill of being with Bri wore off, I remembered what I liked most." He cast an earnest expression at her. "You were the one who kept my interest."

She sucked in a quiet, fluttery breath and held it. If he only knew the pain he had caused because of his change of heart.

"I did things ass backwards, Anne. I should have broken off with Bri first—" with gazes fused, he took another step toward her "—but when I kissed you, I meant it."

She sighed, remembering the whole damn thing. The worst timing in the world, the cringe-worthy thoughts that she'd betrayed her best friend by loving Jack. But damn it, she'd seen him first, that hadn't stopped Brianna from flirting with him, from taking him away from her. And she'd let her. She'd settled for sidekick status. So who was she supposed to blame?

"I'm sorry," he said.

She gave a nod, speechless, needing time to think things through. Nothing had mattered once Brianna got leukemia. And what if he had broken off with Bri and they'd started dating and *then* they'd found out about her diagnosis? Truth was, things were better the way they'd worked out. Some things were never meant to be. Anne's thoughts spun tightly as old guilt weaved through each one, and she worried her head might explode.

Jack took a step closer. "There's one more thing I need to clarify," he said.

She glanced into his eyes, felt heat like hot summer wind cover her as he swept her closer with a strong grasp around the waist, and kissed her neck again. His warm lips pressed hard against the fleshy curve of her shoulder. Sparks flew in all directions, across her chest, up her scalp, down her thighs. Her head tingled as he slowly worked soft kisses up her neck, dipping beneath her hair, lingering there, doubling the chill factor. He nipped her earlobe then moved to her mouth pressing his warm lips to hers just long enough to make her wish for more. It ended far too quickly. With one brief kiss he'd paralyzed her on the spot, stopped her breathing and made her dizzy with pleasure. She reached for his face and pulled him to her mouth to finish a proper kiss. He took back the reins and planted a firm kiss on her mouth that took the last of her breath away.

"*That's* a kiss, speedy," he said, as he released her and strode to his car.

There wasn't a chance in hell she'd be sleeping tonight. At the moment, she couldn't even breathe, and someone was going to have to pry her from this spot. Bart?

Anne steered clear of Jack when he came to help in the morning. She hung out in the kitchen and let her mother take him down to the master bedroom. She'd made sure to get up early enough to be completely dressed when he'd arrived, and through her lethargic eyes, she watched a certain spring in his step as he waved the Spock wave to her with that knowing and damned charming look, and continued down the hall.

Worn out, she'd dutifully returned the sign, having to work a little harder at splitting her fingers two and two.

She leaned against the counter and nursed her first cup of coffee, on alert in case he needed her help. She'd lain awake wishing things could have been different, but knowing life rarely granted a do-over. Jack had held her heart captive all these years by the simple fact that she could never have him. He'd established himself in Whispering Oaks as she had in Portland, and common sense warned her of the likelihood of a super-long-distance relationship lasting. He'd been kissing her like he was interested in having a relationship but she couldn't seriously consider it. Not now, and not with his track record at staying in touch.

Their timing still sucked.

A few minutes later, Jack wheeled her father down the hall. Dad may have been bleary-eyed and disheveled, but he was dressed for his day of leisure.

"God, I need some coffee," he bellowed with Bart at his side looking as if he'd bring it to him if he could figure out what *it* was.

Anne set to work pouring three mugs and passing them around. She'd remembered from all their meetings at Denny's that Jack liked enough cream to make his coffee caramel colored.

"Thanks," he said, sending a private look her way, one that communicated his appreciation but also brought back last night's kisses and the total confusion that followed.

She didn't buy his excuse for dating Bri, but would always love him for sticking by Bri's side until the end.

"No problem." She studied her clunky pink slippers, the one thing she'd forgotten to change, and let a tiny smile tickle the corners of her mouth.

Anne tried to prepare herself, knowing it would be a long day what with getting Lucas's room ready and keeping her parents under control, Jack out of her mind, and not to mention three meals plus extra grocery shopping for Lucas's G.I.-size appetite.

"Well, I've gotta run," Jack said, rinsing his mug and leaving it in the sink, sending a quick glance at Anne as he left.

Anne almost wished he'd stick around as backup, but knew the consequences would be more awkward moments where she'd be bursting to get down to that conversation they both knew needed to be had, to the heart of their old friendship and thwarted budding romance. With Lucas coming home and with her exit back to Oregon in sight, she figured they'd never have a chance to delve any deeper. Maybe it was best left that way.

Her parents said goodbye to him and she waved, thinking twice about walking him out again. He'd apologized, but it had just skimmed the surface. There was so much more to say, and so many more things to figure out. And so little time to do it.

Jocelyn tapped on the back door late that afternoon. "Hi, Annie! Jack told me Lucas is coming home tomorrow."

"Yeah, you want to come with me to pick him up at LAX? You know what a zoo it is, especially on Friday night."

She practically jumped up and down. "I'd love to, but do you think it's safe to leave your parents alone?"

"Good point. Mom's fine, but I'm not sure about Dad."

"Maybe I can sit with them, and Jack can go with you to the airport."

The thought of being alone in a car with Jack for an hour-and-a-half drive to the airport made Anne quake in her flip-flops. "Nah, I'll be fine on my own."

She so wanted to do something, just one thing, without needing Jack's help, but truth was, they all needed him…until Lucas got home.

"He told me to tell you he's available." Jocelyn looked so sincere. "Really, he wants to."

Anne knew she could drive to LAX on her own and get her brother, but did she really want to? It would be so much easier doing it with Jack. Anne fished out her cell phone and sent him a text message.

Truth was, once Lucas got home, they wouldn't need Jack anymore. He could disappear, and she really wasn't sure she wanted him to.

# GET 2 BOOKS

We'd like to send you two *Harlequin® Special Edition* novels absolutely free. Accepting them puts you under no obligation to purchase any more books.

## HOW TO GET YOUR
## 2 FREE BOOKS AND 2 FREE GIFTS

1. Return the reply card today, and we'll send you two *Harlequin Special Edition* novels, absolutely free! We'll even pay the postage!

2. Accepting free books places you under no obligation to buy anything, ever. Whatever you decide, the free books and gifts are yours to keep, free!

3. We hope that after receiving your free books you'll want to remain a subscriber, but the choice is yours- to continue or cancel, any time at all!

## EXTRA BONUS

**You'll also get two free mystery gifts!**
**(worth about $10)**

# FREE!

Return this card today to get
**2 FREE BOOKS and 2 FREE GIFTS!**

 **Harlequin**®

## SPECIAL EDITION

**YES!** Please send me 2 FREE *Harlequin® Special Edition*
novels, and 2 FREE mystery gifts as well. I understand
I am under no obligation to purchase anything, as
explained on the back of this insert.

### 235/335 HDL FMKU

*Please Print*

| | |
|---|---|
| FIRST NAME | LAST NAME |

ADDRESS

| | |
|---|---|
| APT.# | CITY |

STATE/PROV.     ZIP/POSTAL CODE

Visit us at:
www.ReaderService.com

▶ DETACH AND MAIL CARD TODAY! ▶

**BUSINESS REPLY MAIL**
FIRST-CLASS MAIL    PERMIT NO. 717    BUFFALO, NY

POSTAGE WILL BE PAID BY ADDRESSEE

**THE READER SERVICE**
PO BOX 1867
BUFFALO NY 14240-9952

NO POSTAGE
NECESSARY
IF MAILED
IN THE
UNITED STATES

## Chapter Seven

As arranged on Friday, Jack pulled into the driveway at 5:00 p.m. sharp for the trip to the airport. He'd been showing up like clockwork at night in time to put Dad to bed, and again in the morning to get him back up. She'd given him coffee and said very little this morning other than, *see you tonight.*

Anne slipped inside his sedan feeling like she used to, excited and a tiny bit edgy.

"What's this?" she said, pointing to a small cooler on the floor at her feet.

He tossed her a mischievous glance as he backed out of the driveway. "Snacks."

She laughed, and peeked inside: Chips, sodas, candy bars—all his favorites from high school. Something else caught her attention, a package of sour gummy worms, her all time preferred nonfood, nonnutritious "snack."

Silly as it was, his remembering her junk food fave gave her a warm feeling inside as she sniffed the bag. It smelled like raspberry fruit Jell-O powder. Mmm mmm.

"Looks more like we're going on a road trip."

"With the rush hour traffic on the 405, it may seem like one. A very slow road trip."

"Can we start now, or do we have to wait until we get on the freeway?"

"Be my guest. Hey, pop an orange soda for me while you're in there, okay?"

They pulled onto the freeway, nibbling on their treats, chatting away, as if transported back in time to high school...*before* their happy-go-lucky days got pummeled by hard-core life.

He turned on the radio to an oldies station blaring a Smash Mouth song. They looked at each other and blurted out the lyrics. "Might as well be walking on the sun." Anne did her nerd-girl dance, the one that used to crack up Jack, and he bobbed his head in time to the cool electric piano beat.

"Did you know, back then, this was my dad's favorite song, too?"

Jack flashed her a look.

"He said it reminded him of the Doors from the sixties."

"Your dad's a character," he said with a smile. "I

never realized it until I started working with him. He scared the hell out of me in high school."

A common misunderstanding about Anne's father was that he was mean, and scary, which used to embarrass her. She worried that if people didn't like her dad, they'd hate her by association.

"He could be intense at track practice and meets, and with his slacker science students. He's big, loud and overbearing sometimes, but really, he's always been a cuddly teddy bear."

"I know that now, but back then?" Jack shuddered.

"Remember how he used you as a good example to the team because you didn't smoke like half the other kids?"

Jack nodded. "Hell, there was no way I would have smoked."

"It seemed like everyone else did. Was it because you were health conscious?" That didn't seem right. Jack used to consume huge amounts of junk food, and he'd never met a pizza he didn't like.

"That wasn't it," he said, eyes trained on the freeway and the traffic. "My mother smoked."

*Oh, jeez, that's probably why she died. Of course he wouldn't take it up.* "I see. I'm sorry, Jack."

"No need for you to apologize."

"Mom is going bonkers waiting for Lucas to get home. You know how mothers are." Oh, crap, she'd blown it. Hadn't she already put her foot in her mouth by making him talk about his mother, even though she'd died when he was so young? "I'm sorry," she said again. "I forgot."

He glanced at her. "No problem. Really. I'm long over that."

How did someone get over losing a parent?

He cleared his throat. "Remember when I told you my mother died when I was twelve?"

She nodded.

"I lied."

"What?"

"Yeah. I lied. She left me and my dad."

"You mean they got divorced?"

"No. She just up and left. Told my dad she'd done her part and now it was his turn. She didn't want to be his wife anymore or my mother, I guess."

Anne sat reeling at the thought of a mother abandoning her child. She couldn't possibly know both sides of the story, but from where she sat, it was inexcusable. She wasn't sure how to respond to the news, so she sat quietly and hoped he'd open up. She'd had two happily married parents who made no attempt to hide their affections in front of the "kids" and who still made each other smile. She'd been very fortunate. And Jack had gotten quiet.

"That must have hurt you so much."

"She didn't want to be a mother, my mother, anymore. I hated her for it, so I told everyone she'd died."

"Oh, Jack." Her hand flew to his arm. "I had no idea." She wanted to throw her arms around his neck and take the hurt away. She wanted to promise him that one day there'd be someone for him who wouldn't walk away. The thump in her heart took her breath away.

He glanced at her, freeway lights making his face red and sparkly. "I tried to find her. I wrote my Nana, but she hadn't heard from her, and I wrote my Aunt Lori, but she said she didn't know anything, either. I asked my dad to help me find her, but he said it was better just to let her go. After a few years, I found out she'd remarried. She'd run off with some guy she'd only known for a month. Made me feel like I didn't mean anything to her."

Tears brimmed. Anne choked on her anger. "I can't imagine. Oh, Jack."

"I guess that's why I enjoy your parents so much."

"My parents are…well, let's just say they're special." She made a mental note to never complain about them again.

"They're more than special, Anne. They kind of saved my life."

Had Jack needed his life saved? She wondered how bad things had gotten over the past twelve years. Jack seemed to have pulled out of his slump after Brianna died, he'd traveled, gone back to school, now he was a teacher and said he liked the job. And he gave back to the community by volunteering as a firefighter. It seemed more like Jack had saved his own life.

"Sometimes I feel like an orphan, but Kieran and Beverly don't give me a chance. Dad's moved to Orange County to a retirement village, and I don't get to see him as much as I'd like." He glanced at her, then back to the road. "Your parents have filled in the blanks in my life. Anyway, I just wanted to come clean with that. I've felt guilty about lying to you."

"It's completely understandable."

He glanced at her again. "I say this because I don't have a relationship with my mother, so I guess I kind of envy Lucas with your mom going bonkers, as you say, over his coming home and all."

"I see. You've got a good point." Her heart had twisted so tight it was hard to breathe. If she could make all his loss disappear, she would in a heartbeat.

"Hey, I've got a great idea," he said. "Let's change the subject—even though I brought it up."

"Fine with me." Jack had opened up to her. He'd shared a deep secret, which meant he trusted her. The thought of him trusting her made her want to hug him, again. Why did she keep having the urge to throw her arms around him?

Following his cue, she decided to keep things light, and brought up the latest action movie she'd seen. Jack went along with her segue leaving the hurtful subject behind, but the pain lingered in the car like stale cigarette smoke.

Jack went on about how old Stallone looked in the movie, but how he still did his own stunts and how you had to respect him for that.

Safely away from old secrets, she watched Jack's sharp profile as he talked. She savored her umpteenth gummy worm, enjoying how it went from tart to sweet on her tongue, and remembered how thoughtful Jack was to bring them.

Anne was quite sure she'd never get tired of looking at him. His close-cropped hair haloed a well-shaped head, and his strong jaw and nose silhouetted against the night left no doubt that he was an impressively good-looking man. Her pulse went fluttery at the sight, and her heart ached knowing he'd once been hurt so much that he'd lied about his mother leaving him.

"Getting back on topic from last night," he said. "I'd still like to take you away for a day, especially if you plan on leaving for Portland any time soon."

"It would be nice, Jack, but I just don't know if I'll be able to swing it."

He turned sharply. "Try."

She lifted her brows. "I'll see."

He looked back to the freeway.

"You gonna send Jocelyn over to do your dirty work again?"

He laughed, but didn't say another word.

What would be the point of spending more time with him? It would be stupid to get a taste of being with him again only to go home to her routine. Jack didn't have a place in her life anymore. But damn, being next to him in the car, smelling his distinct scent, seeing the same expressions she'd loved when they were teens, was more than tempting. For the rest of her life she'd associate Jack with the smell of gummy worms.

Being near him felt like sugarcoated torture.

Song after song looped through the radio, each

with a different memory as they exited the freeway and drove down Sepulveda Boulevard heading for the airport.

"Are you excited about seeing Lucas?"

"I can't wait. It's hard to believe he'll be home for good now."

"Yeah, like you said, your mom's practically levitating she's so happy."

"As far as kid brothers go, he's a good guy. I've always liked him." She had a quick flashback of being around eight and Lucas around six with their arms locked, playing wrestlers. He was determined to beat Anne, though younger and definitely scrawnier. Anne took him down as fast as she could. He fought all the way and hit his head hard on the grass but refused to cry. She'd admired him for that.

The next memory jumped forward to when she was a junior in high school, sitting in the torn bucket seat of his prized junker '64 Mustang, the car he wouldn't be old enough to drive for another year, not that it would be drivable by then. She was whining about Jack asking out Brianna on a date. Lucas had kept working on the engine, but he'd let her put it all out there. Every single feeling she couldn't tell anyone else in the world, she'd lain on Lucas, and he hadn't even complained. That was something else she admired about him. Yeah, she'd missed her kid brother all these years.

Her cell rang and when she saw it was Lucas, her fingers tingled. "Hey, what's up?"

"I'm here. Waiting for my bag."

"Okay, we're about ten minutes away. Be on the lookout for a blue Audi, since Jack's driving."

"Who's Jack?"

"You know, Jack from high school. Jack of Jack and Bri?"

It took a second, but must have sunk in. "Oh. Yeah."

"Just be ready, and we'll get you at the curb."

"Nah, I'll wait at the van and bus pickup instead. It'll make it easier for you."

She knew the inner lane, the one you were supposed to pick up people at, was a circus and a nightmare to navigate and a total time suck, and Lucas mustn't have wanted them to get stuck in a traffic jam or risk a fender bender in the black hole of terminal six.

"That's no problem," she said. "We'll be fine picking you where we're supposed to."

"Hey, here's my bag, I'm heading for the van curb. See you there."

There was never any point to arguing with Lucas once he'd made up his mind. That was definitely one aspect of his personality she hadn't always admired.

"Okay, but be ready to jump in the car."

He clicked off. She turned to Jack. "Remember that time we picked Brianna's dad up after his trip to Vegas?" Her parents were divorced and he'd pop in and out of Bri's life.

Jack thought for a moment then nodded. "You mean the drive-by thing where we almost got a ticket?"

"That's how Lucas wants to do it."

"He's my kind of guy." Jack grinned.

What was it with men?

As they approached the airport, the traffic thickened. Horns honked and cars swerved in and out of lanes, jockeying for the best spot. A river of white lights trailed behind and red lights preceded them.

"Thank you for doing this, Jack. This part always makes me crazy."

"No problem," he said, with a teasing tone. "I like a challenge."

Anne watched for her brother as they got closer. A cacophony of noise hit her when she opened her window and stuck her head outside. The screech of brakes and horns seemed never ending. Irritated shouts rose over the racket. Exhaust fumes threatened to overtake her.

In the near distance, an imposing figure standing at ease in military fashion, stood on the ready. He wore denims and desert-colored military boots, with a dark tailored shirt he hadn't bothered to tuck in. Civvies. And his dark hair was longer than she'd seen it in years. He'd finally finished his military commitment.

Lucas had bulked up even more since she'd last seen him, and it seemed he'd grown another inch or two. No more little brother, but all man.

"Lucas!" she called. "Lucas!"

His head pivoted toward the car. He waved at her and grabbed his duffle bag, just as they pulled to the curb. The car on their tail laid into their horn, and came to a stop with a long nerve-racking howl. A bus with the squeakiest brakes in the world pulled up behind, making her wonder if it might rear-end the other car and cause a chain reaction.

"Get in!" she called, unlocking the door.

Lucas tore open the back door, threw his bag into the seat and dove inside.

"Go, Jack, go!" Anne said, once the passenger door was closed.

Like a pro, Jack swerved into the next lane and took off as fast as the traffic allowed, leaving the unhappy driver stuck between a bus and a double-parked hotel shuttle van with a line of passengers boarding. Anne felt terrible but quickly forgot as she turned toward her brother in the backseat.

"Lucas!"

"Hey, Annie," Lucas said as he buckled in. He'd always called her Annie after she'd fibbed and explained to him at the ripe old age of seven that Mom and Dad had named her Anne with an E because it was more special than just plain old Ann. Just like the book her mom had read to her then, *Anne of Green Gables*.

"I can't believe you're here!" she said, reaching over the seat to take his hand, wishing she'd been able to at least jump out and hug him.

He smiled at her, but it didn't reach his eyes, as he squeezed her hand briefly, then let go, glancing toward Jack. "Hey, man, thanks for the ride."

"You're welcome. I haven't had this much fun since playing chicken in my uncle's pickup truck," Jack said, as they edged their way out of the airport and back toward the freeway. "Want a cola?"

That got a near smile out of Lucas.

"Mom and I made your favorite cake."

"Sweet."

By the time they'd arrived back home, they'd covered all possible small talk about the airplane ride, the food, the weather plus Mom and Dad's situation. Lucas answered everything when asked, but Anne couldn't help but feel he was careful to keep his distance. It made her sad to think they'd slipped so far apart over the past nine years.

After a quick stop at home, where Lucas hopped out of the backseat, withdrew his duffel bag, and gave a few more niceties and thank-yous to Jack, Anne walked around to the driver's side to say goodbye to Jack as Lucas headed for the front door.

"Thanks again," she said.

"I told you, I was glad to do it."

His unwavering eyes caught her off guard. How did he do that?

Her mother's squeal of joy could be heard all the way to the street. "Lucas! I can't believe it's you!" It made Anne smile.

"I'd get up and hug you, son, but I can't!" she heard her father's loud voice say, and almost laughed.

"There's a couple of happy campers," Jack said with a wistful smile.

"You want to come in for some cake?"

"Nah. This reunion should just be family."

She nodded, appreciating his consideration. "Well,

I've got to go inside," she said, her eyes cast toward the house and the bustle of activity within.

"Okay. Call me if you need me."

"Will do, but Lucas should be able to manage all the muscle stuff now."

He reached out and took her hand. "Give some thought to Sunday."

So distracted by his touch, she had to stop and think in order to remember what he'd said. "I'll see what happens." She let go of his grasp and started to walk away, torn over how to deal with his offer, and wishing he didn't mix up her mind so easily.

Jack shifted the car into Reverse. Why had he never gone after her in Oregon?

Because he was afraid to find out she hadn't felt the same way about him that he had about her. It was as simple as that. She'd shut down so drastically as soon as Bri had gotten sick, he didn't know what to think. Then, after Bri had died, she'd left town. Left him.

Yet every minute he'd spent with her since she'd been home seemed to re-cement that long-ago bond they'd shared. Back in high school, if he'd get too big for his Nikes, she'd cut him back down to size. If she'd get too self-conscious about her appearance, he'd tell her to get over it. That she was fine the way she was. He'd confess he felt stupid in trig, and she'd reassure him he was the coolest guy in school. She'd whine about her family and he'd tease her that she should have been named *Me Me Me Me*.

Tonight, driving to the airport, felt like all the times the three of them used to go to the beach, or Universal CityWalk, or to the orange groves at the edge of Marshfield where all the high school kids secretly met to hang out. He shook his head and smiled remembering one time when Anne had started a capture-the-flag game in the groves with only the moon for light. Somehow, with Anne, everything turned into an adventure. He liked it and he wanted more.

Drew had told him to apologize so he could move on. Well, he had apologized and where had that moving on led—right back to Anne.

If he could just get her alone, have the luxury of spending an entire day with her, where he could work up the guts to tell her how he still felt.

*Take a chance with me, Anne. Let's see where things lead.*

Was it so crazy to hold on to a dream?

He could fly to Portland for a weekend here and there, and she could come back to visit. Her family would love that, too. It would just take a little extra effort to have a long-distance relationship. If things worked out.

He drove on lost in his thoughts, weighing the pros and cons of laying it all on the line with Anne. By the time he got off the freeway, he'd come back to reality.

That wasn't how it worked in his life. Women didn't stick around for Jack Lightfoot. Not any women he loved, anyway.

And how could he ever find out if he loved Anne, when she wouldn't even spare him a day?

By the time he'd parked the car in his garage, he'd firmly planted his feet back on the ground. As usual, he'd been foolish to think he could ever have a life with someone to love.

"Give it up, Lightfoot," he said as he slammed the car door.

But his overwhelming desire to be with Anne didn't listen.

Anne couldn't sleep what with all the excitement of having Lucas home, not to mention with her thoughts drifting back over and over to Jack.

Just thinking about being in Jack's arms made her hot. Really hot.

She threw back the covers and walked to the kitchen for a cool drink of water. When she passed Lucas's room the door was ajar, so she peeked inside. He wasn't in bed. She went to the sink, filled her cup and glanced out the window. The side entrance to the garage was open and through the door, she could tell there was a dim light on. She took a few swallows, left her glass and followed the light.

Making her way around the house, trying not to wake up Bart, and out the patio door, she almost tripped on a brick in the yard. She steadied herself and walked over to the driveway to the detached three-car garage, and to the opened side entry door.

Anne entered quietly.

Inside she found Lucas in army-brown boxers, looking over his Mustang. He'd almost completely rebuilt it before he'd left for the service.

The broadness of his shoulders and chest, plus the cut of his arms surprised her. So did the large tattoo on his back of a raven perched on each shoulder. Dad would hit the ceiling when he discovered that.

Lucas glanced at her. "I can't believe Dad kept this around."

"I think he knew you'd come after him if he ever tried to sell it." She smiled, her attempt at humor falling flat. When had Lucas gotten so serious?

Except for the one work light over the car, the cavernous garage was filled with deep shadows and black contours like those ravens on his back, places for bogeymen to hide, or haunting thoughts to hover.

"What are you doing up?" she asked.

"I can't sleep."

"Maybe it's jet lag?"

He made a halfhearted laugh. "Yeah, maybe that's it."

Thick grease and oil fumes made Anne a little nauseated. She wanted to leave, wasn't sure Lucas wanted her around anyway.

"Can I bring you anything from the kitchen?"

"I'm fine, Annie. Thanks."

He'd gone along with all the hoopla earlier. Mom couldn't quit hugging him or bringing up silly childhood incidents. Dad had pummeled him with military questions. He ate the cake and seemed happy enough to be home, but Anne couldn't help thinking a lot went on under the surface.

Troubled by her brother's sullenness, she wanted to stick around and force him to talk, to be the goofy kid brother she'd once had, but he seemed resolute in his silence, and she'd respect that for now. Besides, her bed called out, and she really was tired, so she waved good-night. "I'm going back inside."

"Okay, I'll see you in the morning."

Anne hoped tomorrow, which would usher in the sun in a few short hours, would bring Lucas back to the family. On her walk to the house, she noticed the light on in the upper bedroom next door. Jocelyn's old room. The same room she'd been staying in since housesitting for her parents while they drove across country in their new RV. Why was she up at this hour?

When Anne crawled back under the covers, she noticed the light on her cell phone. There was a text from Jack. Come away with me on Sunday?

What was he still doing up? Maybe some weird insomnia gas had been sprinkled over the Generation Y crowd of Whispering Oaks. Maybe it was the hour or the lack of sleep, but Jack had asked several times now, and not replying would be downright rude.

She used her thumbs to type out her answer. OK.

## Chapter Eight

Saturday morning when Kieran was ready to get up, Anne tapped lightly on Lucas's bedroom door. "Sorry to bug you, but we need help with Dad." She suspected he'd been out in the garage most of Friday night.

Lucas opened the door looking bleary-eyed. His hair came together on top of his head in an accidental faux hawk. "I'll be right there," he said, with a low smoky voice.

He hopped to attention, threw on a T-shirt, and strode across the hall to his parents' room. Bart hadn't warmed up to Lucas yet, and sat whining several feet away from the bed, anxiously watching his master and warily eyeing the new guy.

"Well, good morning, bright eyes!" her father said,

using the old term for any of his kids who didn't look alert and on top of the world at the breakfast table.

Kieran had already managed to get himself into a sitting position at the edge of the bed. It had to have been by sheer will if his wrinkled brow, ruffled hair and twisted bedsheets were any indication.

"Hey, Dad," Lucas said, sounding unfazed. "So how do we do this?"

Mom had already thrown a bright yellow robe over her shoulders and stood close by to guide Lucas through the process. In the middle of her explanation on how to get Dad into the wheelchair with the leg extension, and what worked and what didn't, Anne's cell phone rang.

Lucas nodded at her. "I can take it from here. Go ahead and answer."

Anne scooted down the hall, noting the call was from her boss. "Hello?"

"Hi, Anne, it's Jessica. I was wondering if you had an update on when you'll be coming back to work?"

Anne had been avoiding the timeline. Originally she'd promised it wouldn't take more than two weeks, since she hadn't been working there long enough to earn vacation pay, but Lucas's army discharge had gotten postponed. Now she was onto the fourth week and even though Lucas was home, for some reason, which probably began with the letter *J*, she was dragging her feet about making departure plans.

"Oh. Well, my brother got home last night, and my dad has his first post-op appointment this coming Wednesday. I'd like to be there for the update on his progress. Would it be okay if I start Monday after next?" She hoped her pocketbook could handle another week without pay.

"I think we can make due for one more week. But I'm going to have to ask you to promise you'll be here then. I'll tell the nurse registry that we won't need them after this week."

"Okay, great, thanks so much," she said as a glum feeling settled in. "I will definitely be there." She should be grateful to have that job in Portland, shouldn't she? She'd gotten burned out in the hospital, and this clinic kept her up to date on medicine while giving her a chance to do administrative work, too. She liked what she did…usually.

"Things have been a little rocky without you, and even Dr. Khatebe says he misses you!"

Anne laughed, knowing, of all the doctors she worked for, he was the hardest to please and prone to tantrums. "You tell him I'll be back!"

And she would. She'd seen her parents through the worst of their accident, her mother was set to go back to school with the help of a room aide, and her father was settling into his routine without all the griping. He understood healing took time, and he would have to wait it out. Most importantly, Lucas was home and he could take over with the heavy labor. Mom would have to figure out how to do her own hair, and it wouldn't kill her to microwave a meal now and then. Or maybe Lucas had learned to cook? Miracles could happen.

Heck, if she could take care of three squares a day for her parents, so could he.

So that took care of her family.

One last disturbing thought drew her brows together. Jack.

By Sunday morning, the infamous Whispering Oaks wind had whipped itself into frenzy mode. Dry heat blew through the valley displacing leaves and twigs, and messing with everyone's hair.

The weather matched Anne's tempestuous emotions over her date with Jack. Guilt led the march. She'd awakened earlier that morning with thoughts of Brianna. How her friend had truly loved Jack, and how it occurred to Anne that Jack was the only man Brianna had ever had the chance to love. And Anne's heart nearly broke recalling the look of desperation on her best friend's face when she'd told Anne she thought Jack had found someone else—this, only days before Jack kissed Anne, and a week before Brianna got sick.

When Brianna told Anne she'd seen Jack kiss a girl behind the oak tree, she panicked that she'd seen who it was, but Brianna had given no indication she had, only that she'd seen Jack and then she'd run off in tears. Keeping her secret made Anne feel like the world's biggest heel. Sometimes she still did.

She packed a hat and put her hair in a ponytail in order to keep it out of her face. Maybe it wouldn't be so windy wherever they were going. Though filled with mixed feelings about spending the day with Jack, she overrode her private protests and went all out. She powdered and blushed then touched up her eyes with mascara and a pale plum line on her bottom lid, then chose lipstick to match her outfit. She dotted herself with the fruity orange flower and jasmine scent of Secret Obsession, and chose the nicest top she'd packed on that last moments' notice four weeks back. The raspberry-colored, split-neck knit dipped low enough to show the lace on her white camisole. And that sheer lace matched her skimpy underwear, not that anyone would be seeing hers today.

For comfort, she picked her black stretch jeans and flats. And for a little pizzazz, she chose a long necklace made from teardrop-shaped rose quartz beads.

She slipped on a matching ring and noticed her fingers trembled. Guilt stabbed at the smile she practiced for the mirror.

She was sick of it. Sick and tired of dragging around the baggage that had defined the three of them and that damned deadly diagnosis. But she was alive and Brianna had only just made it to her eighteenth birthday. Survivor guilt. Usually she didn't let it affect her this way, but every now and then the old guilt came up and slapped her hard, like today. Maybe it was the time spent with Jack lately that brought it all up. She'd thought she'd worked through the feelings years ago, but, surprise! Here they were again.

Nope. She wasn't going to go down that tired old path. Not today. She'd deal with it once and for always.

One last glance in the mirror and with new resolve,

she pulled loose her ponytail then brushed out her hair. Jack used to comment how he liked her hair down. Well, guess what, she liked it best that way, too. To hell with the wind.

Without being obvious, she wanted to look extra nice for her first—and most likely last—date with Jack Lightfoot.

Anne recognized the rhythmic knock with the straggling *tap tap*. With a fluttering heart and a brisk butterfly run through her innards, she rushed from the family room and opened the door for Jack.

He stood there with a silly grin on his face, looking like the devil in a muted green polo shirt and jeans. She studied him, taking in every detail. Fern green eyes surrounded by thick brown lashes. Freshly shaved face. Dark blond hair with the hint of product on board.

Anne didn't speak.

Neither did he.

They smiled at each other for a few seconds.

"So," he finally said.

"So." She nodded, twisting the hem on her top.

"You look great."

"Thanks." *So do you!*

"You ready?"

A gust of wind stirred across the yard whipping up leaves into a mini twister of the same magnitude as her nerves. Was she ready for their date?

"Yep." Not really! "Let me get my things."

At nine o'clock on this lazy Sunday morning, and

with Kieran and Lucas still in bed, Beverly wandered into the room. "There's my hero! Hi, Jack."

"Hey, Bev."

She headed toward the door for a quick chat as Anne went down the hall.

"Bev" touched Anne's arm when she reemerged from her bedroom then passed in the hall. She carried a cup of coffee and Anne knew it was for her father. Out of earshot from Jack, Bev whispered, "I hope you have a great day."

Her parents had been very good about keeping this "date" with Jack low-key, as if they understood she might bolt over the slightest infringement on her privacy. Of course, they'd only found out about it yesterday, and with her thumb on the pulse of her parents' attitude concerning Jack Lightfoot, she knew they were both solidly in his camp.

Anne could read a thousand wishes in her mother's expression as she said goodbye. It's time to find a guy. Move back to Whispering Oaks. Settle down. Get married. Make a family. He's the one. She mentally plugged her ears and sang *la la la la*. If only she could shield those telepathic maternal thoughts, but noooo. Right there in the hallway they came through loud and clear, nearly reverberating off the walls.

Anne couldn't let her mind drift in that direction. By next weekend, she'd have a date with a plane for home.

They made a run for the car. Her hair didn't stand a chance.

Once she got inside and Jack slid behind the wheel,

she could smell his tried and true Irish Spring, and loved the spicy citrusy scent. His pheromones sent a low-level electrical hum throughout her body whether she wanted it or not. Would she be able to withstand this feeling all day, or would his natural charm wear her down?

She glanced over at him digging in his pocket for the car key, and noticed his thick thigh and natural bulge in his jeans. The constant hum upgraded to zing and in order to control her reaction, she looked away on a quiet inhale. The answer was in, no way would she be able to resist him an entire day.

"Thought I'd take you to my favorite place for breakfast," he said, while starting the car.

Would she even be able to eat? "Great. I'm starved." How many more lies would she tell today?

They drove down the street with wind licking the windows and jostling the car.

"I haven't seen it this bad in a long time," she said. Anything to break the silence.

"Yeah, it's sort of like freakishly out-of-season Santa Anas. I'm hoping we'll drive out of this mess when we get to the coast."

"I'd love to see the ocean today."

"I thought we'd head up to Santa Barbara, what do you say?"

"I'm in!"

Ten minutes later, Jack pulled into a driveway. "We're here."

"I thought we were going for breakfast?"

"And you're right." He gestured toward the town house. "My favorite breakfast place. Come on inside and see. I've got everything just about ready."

Excitement chills made the hair on her arms stand up, and the unwanted reaction forced her to realize how big a deal their day together would be. He'd already gone out of his way to make it special by cooking for her. That thought made her stomach tighten to crunch level.

Walking into Jack's house felt a bit like falling down Alice's rabbit hole. It had been hard enough dealing with the different sides of Jack, the man and the teenager, over the past few weeks. Now, he'd soundly morphed into a man, and his home and furnishings proved it. This was the side of Jack she'd worried about most—the irresistibly appealing side.

A brown leather sectional couch invited her to take her shoes off and sink into the soft cushions. It sat in the center of the room, helping to delineate the living area from the kitchen. Expensive looking tan-colored tile covered both rooms, with a dark patterned area rug breaking up the potential monotony. His taste in bright-colored wall art surprised her. For bachelor living, the room seemed balanced and inviting...just like Jack— the adult version.

Something else was awfully inviting—the aroma of potatoes and sausage and cheese. "Wow, whatever you cooked smells great!"

He smiled, excitement darkening his eyes. He opened the sliding glass door and escorted her onto a small balcony. "I thought we'd eat out here. Have a seat."

She did as she was told, and noticed that the three-quarter sheltered area blocked out most of the pervading wind. He'd already set the table. She smiled at the ultra trendy square, cappuccino-brown stoneware plates and fun squiggly handles on the flatware, and the functional yet classy place settings.

The thought of Jack taking the time to pick out such specific utensils both surprised her and reminded her how little she knew him anymore. It also made her wonder if a woman had participated in helping him pick out his dishes, and an odd territorial thread stitched through her body.

He interrupted her thoughts by bringing out an already cut and sectioned ruby red grapefruit half.

"Thanks!"

He sat beside her with his own. "You're welcome. I'm letting the casserole cool a bit."

"When did you become Mr. Domestic?"

"When I grew up. How about you?"

"Um," she said in between juicy bites, "when it became a necessity."

He smiled and touched her hand. "I'm really glad you're here. Oh, and I've got something for you."

He reached behind him on the patio counter for a large brown envelope and handed it to her.

"What's this?"

"I did some research on the internet for you and printed out a bunch of stuff."

Beyond curious, Anne opened the envelope and took out the contents. *RN to M.D.* the heading read. She gave him a questioning glance.

"You said you always wanted to be a doctor, and well, I looked into what it takes to go from RN to M.D." He paused, his look intent. "Since your MCAT scores are only good for three years, you'd have to retake them. Oh, and..." He reached over and took the papers from her and searched for something. "See this?" He pointed to a list. "This program guarantees to take a person with a Bachelors of Science in Nursing and fix them up with the missing sciences you'd need. Mostly they're advanced chemistry courses and stuff like that, which I know you're good at because you saved my neck in Chem 101." He gave a heartwarming grin. "And they guarantee to have you ready to apply to med school in one year."

Dumbfounded, Anne stared at Jack. He'd gone out of his way to research and reopen her long lost dream of becoming a doctor. She didn't know whether to kiss him for being so sweet, or scream in terror that he was calling her bluff. Did she still have the passion she'd once had to become a doctor? She'd been thinking of going back to school and didn't know why, but maybe Jack had nailed it for her.

"They offer an intense study course to prepare you for taking the MCATs, too. What do you think?"

Anne shook her head. "This is amazing, Jack. I can't believe you did all this for me."

"I wanted to. After our talk at the hospital, I thought

maybe you'd still be interested. You wouldn't even have to leave home because this program helps you find the courses you need at local state universities, and they'll assist with applications to medical schools, even make you do practice essays. All kinds of stuff."

"I think you're more excited about this than I am." She smiled, sensing caution interfere with her elation.

"I want you to be happy, Anne. I think this falls under the things-I-really-wanted-to-do-but-didn't category."

Speaking of things she really wanted to do…she studied Jack, nearly melting from the feverish sincerity in his eyes. "This is so sweet. Thank you." Jack's interest in her interrupted education had taken her by surprise, but the time and effort he'd put into researching the program reached all the way inside and touched her soft spot. So moved, she fought off a subtle urge to cry. "I promise to read it thoroughly."

He squeezed her shoulder. "Good. I'm glad then." The warmth of his touch sent feathery sensations through her chest.

They spent a lot of time smiling at each other during the first course. Whenever his eyes flicked her way, she made some straight-lined or curvy-lipped response, which wasn't easy while eating. When he got up to remove the dishes, he placed his hand on her shoulder again, and gave another subtle squeeze. "Should I turn on some music?" There went another chill squad.

"Sure."

Even though it was morning, he chose a smoky sax

and piano piece, something that Anne could see listening to on a rainy day. She liked his taste. What would a rainy day with Jack be like? She'd spent so many of them alone in Portland. A million thoughts overwhelmed her as she sat on his balcony, sipping rich brewed coffee, and stared at the bending trees in the nearby yard.

Soon he was back with another shoulder squeeze while setting the casserole on the glass tabletop. The warmth of his palm unsettled her far more than being in his house and watching him dish out their meal.

His domestic touches may have surprised her, but his cooking skills downright shocked her. "This looks fabulous!" The rich, cheesy eggs—plus sausage bits mixed together with grated potato and topped with a crispy hash brown crust—nearly sent her taste buds out of the stratosphere. "I know it can't be good for me."

"You don't need to worry about that, you're in great shape."

"Thanks, but high cholesterol doesn't have anything to do with a person's figure."

"You're right, but let's not think about anything practical right now." The glint in his eye suggested they take a break today. Okay, she could do that. Heck, wasn't it about time? So it was settled then. Today would be a welcomed moratorium on logic and on all things confusing about her and Jack.

*Go with the flow, Anne.* She took a bite and savored the flavor, and after she swallowed said, "This tastes great." She squeezed his forearm to emphasize the point, enjoying the light dusting of hair on his arm.

"Thank you."

There was that earnest gaze again, the one that accompanied his searching eyes every time they looked at each other.

He cleared his throat. "Hey, Anne, you look terrific today, and I'm really glad you're here."

This time their glances met and fused. She clamped down on those fern green eyes and took in every gorgeous detail. There was a darker green ring around the outside of his iris, and there was also a message buried in his stare. No doubt this meal was a peace offering and so far she'd enjoyed every bit of his effort along with each bite. "I'm glad I'm here, too."

That got a smile out of him, as he delicately removed a few strands of hair that a particularly energetic gust of wind, which broke through the barrier, had blown across her face.

"Let me help with the dishes," she said, when they'd finished eating.

"I can do them later."

"The cheese and eggs will be caked on, let me…"

He stopped her with a kiss. It was brief, but was more than enough to startle her and shut her up. She inhaled and opened her eyes to find a victorious grin on his face as he gathered dishes from the table. She took the rest and followed him into the kitchen.

"I've got to tell you, you have a great place here," she said, still recovering from the kiss.

"Thanks. I'll take you on a tour."

"Are you leasing or buying?"

"My dad sold our house and moved into a retirement community and gave me a good chunk of change to put down on a house. With all my school loans, I couldn't have done it without him."

After they scraped and rinsed the dishes and put the remaining casserole in the refrigerator, he guided her with his hand at the small of her back out of the kitchen and down the hall. The warmth of his touch set off feathery tingles up and down her spine. Oh, and there went the fine hair on her arms standing on end again.

They stopped outside the first door. "This is my office-slash-guest-bedroom," Jack said. "Dad comes to visit from time to time, and Drew sleeps here whenever Cindy kicks him out."

Anne laughed remembering the volatile relationship Drew and Cindy had all the way back in high school. The fact that they were still together said something for the power of first love. She glanced at Jack. He bore a soft-lipped smile, and she fought the urge to reach out and touch his mouth. It rattled her.

"And this is the guest bath." He nudged her farther down the hall before she could explore the pint-size room. "This is my bedroom."

He used his eyes and made an arc toward his room. She took a breath and stepped inside. His choice of dark cherry wood furniture was rich and classy, just like him. She tried not to look at the bed too long, though it screamed of masculinity. Foregoing a bedspread, it had been made with military precision, clean white sheets and one pale blue pillow at the center to match the blanket tucked tight enough to bounce a quarter on.

The fluffy white area rug, and the notion that it was the first thing he wiggled his toes on each morning, amused her. It felt too intimate in here. She needed to take a step back, but she bumped into him and his firm, warm chest. Slowly, she turned around and found his eyes. They watched her intently, as if reading her every thought and forcing a few of his naughty notions into the mix.

She needed to get out of here but couldn't make her feet work. He took both of her hands and tugged her closer, clasped her wrists and turned them over. He gazed at her upward-turned palms, as if reading her fortune, as if they were precious gifts and lifted first one, then the other, to his lips for the gentlest of kisses.

The tingle fest now included the hair on the back of her neck. She wasn't ready for this, couldn't begin to handle the thought of going any further.

"I should freshen up before…" Oh, God, that didn't come across the way she'd meant it "—before we leave," she finished quickly and eased her hands out of his grasp.

He watched her antsy reaction while leaning with one hand against the wall, with a curious lift of his brow. "Yeah, I guess I should, too."

They stared at each other far longer than necessary, the air heavy with unspoken thoughts and desires.

A quick jealous jolt took her by surprise. How many

other women had "freshened up" for Jack in his manly-schmanly house? She wanted to kick herself. He was entitled to a life, even if she'd been living like a Buddhist monk, which was probably why being here with Jack had knocked her sideways. She was acting more like a high school girl than a mature woman.

Oh, God, they were still standing in the hall staring at each other. Someone needed to do something. She should step inside the bathroom and close the door.

Why had things gotten so awkward?

She glanced into the adjacent room. Maybe because they stood just outside Jack's bedroom with a clear view of his thick, large, masculine king-size bed?

## Chapter Nine

When Anne stepped out of the guest bathroom, the heat radiating from Jack hadn't decreased a single degree. In fact, he must have rushed over to his master bath and brushed his teeth, since he seemed slightly out of breath with a distinct minty scent.

The pep talk she'd given herself in front of the mirror hadn't helped her nerves a bit.

He used her necklace to tug her toward him, then kissed the tip of her nose. Not the move she'd expected, but she wasn't complaining. It gave her the chance to take in his natural clean-guy smell, something so simple yet such a turn-on.

His hands settled on her hips when he slanted his head and moved in for a real kiss. He took his time pressing moist, minty kisses on her lips—gentle, sweet busses promising so much more that she knotted his shirt in her fists.

He cupped her face, drew her closer and kissed her harder, opening her mouth and slipping his tongue across the inside of her lips. Her mouth tingled under his touch and taste.

Anne settled her hands on Jack's neck, her fingers roaming across the prickly short hair on the back of his head. She rubbed and tugged on his earlobes and he moaned, so she did it again, all the while kissing and coiling tighter and tighter inside.

Jack backed her against the wall, leaned into her and kissed her ear. She nuzzled into his neck, savoring the nearness of him and the welcomed pressure of his body, suddenly hell-bent with desire to be naked and wrapped flush against his skin.

As if sensing her shift, he pulled back, fire in his gaze, a flush on his face and nailed her with a hooded, questioning stare. She answered with a silent, but distinct message—*hell, yeah, I'm ready!* Seeing the willingness in her eyes, he clasped her wrist and led her across the hall to his room. Without protest, she followed.

Unable to stay apart for long, they stopped halfway to the bed. He pivoted, she bumped into him, and they found and devoured each other's mouths again.

She got lost in his mounting kisses. All her doubts shut down allowing her to savor each step of the dance. Beginning with the necklace and her shaky inhale, piece by piece he removed the barriers between them with a playful, sexy glint in his eyes. Now down to her skimpy lace bra and thong, and nearly overcome with the serious turn of his expression—a wondrous look of amazement—she watched as he pulled his shirt over his head. Muscles and flat abs, suntanned with a sprinkling of light hair, made her ache to be with him.

Anne stopped Jack when he went for the snap on his jeans. She placed the flat of her palm equally over the waistband and his stomach, and enjoyed a mild thrill when he sucked in a breath. She glanced up and got another shot of pure adrenaline from his hooded, heat-driven gaze. This job, undressing Jack, was one she'd waited her entire adult life for, and it would be hers and hers alone. The satisfying sound as each snap on his jeans popped open to reveal the silky dark material of his boxers, fanned the wildfire of her longing, and had definitely been worth the wait.

With her bra pressed flat to his chest, she pushed the jeans downward and, maintaining the tight proximity, she accompanied the pants as she slid them over his hips and down his thighs. What had been a promising bulge in his jeans had become unequivocally hard. Jack was ready and more than willing to make love to her. Dizzy with anticipation, the day and moment had finally come.

On her knees, she tugged off his boxers while her heart raced.

Finding it hard to breathe, she sat back on her heels in awe of the total picture of Jackson Lightfoot. He'd finally become her dream…in the flesh. For the rest of her life, she'd never forget his rugged symmetry and masculine perfection...or the indescribable way he looked at her.

The dark longing in his eyes set off a storm of chills so strong, she couldn't move.

Jack picked her up and carried her to the bed then blanketed her with his body. They kissed again and again, as if each kiss were a breath of life. He cupped her breasts, first through the lacy bra and again, after skillfully removing it, as he kissed and suckled each one. Sensations roared over her chest and shoulders heading straight to her center, fully wakening the sex-starved sleeping giant.

"You're beautiful, Anne. I can't believe how beautiful you are."

Under his gaze, her insecurities about her round face and average features disappeared, and she never felt more appealing in her life.

If she could get her mouth to work or her brain to think about something other than the feel of Jack's lips on her breasts, she might have had a shot at a coherent reply. Instead, she focused on the sleek skin of his back, his heat and substance, and how she wanted more and more of him.

"Jack," she said, with a breathy pleading sound.

It must have been the perfect response—all that he needed to come undone.

Unleashed and long overdue, their lovemaking flamed hot and fast with ravenous kisses, desperate grasps, rolling over and under each other, quickly applying the necessary protection and, finally, coupling.

Astounded by the perfect fit and feel of him, his heat and power over her, and the wonder of making love with Jack, she rocked as he thrust. Her response came quick and hard, with all the subtlety of an atomic bomb and mushroom cloud.

She was pretty sure she called out his name again, but the implosion temporarily deafened her. Though not her sense of touch, and from Jack's sudden lunge and halt, she realized he'd detonated, too, sending a whole new hot flowing sensation throughout her core.

A few moments later, interlocked and both collapsed from sensory overload, Jack raised his head.

"I sure as hell gave you the right nickname, speedy," he said with a ragged breath.

She laughed and hid her face against his shoulder. "That's so embarrassing."

"No! No, I meant that in a good way. An incredibly, fantastically, great way." He kissed her neck. The smile beaming from his face was all the further clarification she needed. And for that, he received another long and super energetic kiss.

They showered together and fell into another exploration adventure, ending with more sex. Jack had to hop out of the shower to grab a condom and almost slipped on the wet floor but returned undaunted, wearing nothing but a huge grin and a latex sheath. With one leg wrapped around his waist and the other barely touching the slate-tiled shower floor, she thought this was as close to having stand-up sex as she'd ever come. Good thing he was strong.

Somehow, since his home-cooked breakfast, they'd gone from old friends to hot cookin' lovers. Anne stumbled over the idea as she dried herself. What did it mean? Jack stepped in, wrapped another towel over her shoulders, and finished the job. Could she give up anymore to him and handle the consequences?

The shiver that followed had nothing to do with titillation and everything to do with reality. And doubt. *There's always something missing, Anne.* Maybe this was standard operation for Jack Lightfoot—try the ladies out then back off.

He noticed her prickled skin. "Cold?"

She nodded, and he rubbed faster with the towel, while she contemplated the onslaught of her sudden cold feet.

"I promised you a day by the ocean," he said into her ear, hands on her shoulders, his warm breath showering her with tingles. "And I'm a man of my word, so let's get moving, okay?" He lightly snapped her with the towel when he walked away.

She smiled, though it wasn't genuine. "Yeah, I haven't been to the coast yet this trip. Give me five minutes and I'll be all set."

She combed out her hair, but avoided looking in the steamy mirror, not sure she could handle what she'd see. A woman in love?

It was obvious Jack had been invigorated by their

lovemaking, as he slapped opened and closed closet doors and drawers, while whistling and getting dressed. If only she could be as casual about the whole thing as he was.

With the lust clouds clearing and her mind jumbled with a new onslaught of mixed-up feelings, Anne envied him.

The unseasonal winds had cleared the air and emptied the sky of everything except the sun. Bright blue, three shades lighter than the ocean, it went on forever until the sea joined it on the horizon. The view revitalized Anne, and helped steer her thoughts away from caution and warning.

What was wrong with her? Jack was happy as the dolphins she'd just spied slipping in and out of the breakers off Route 101. His smile should be infectious, but she'd pulled back into herself. How long before he caught on?

No. She wouldn't allow it. Not now. Not during her one chance to be with Jack. She'd dreamed about this day since she'd been sixteen. There he was sitting across from her in the car, the swaggering guy, all proud of himself for making her come, happy to be alive…happy to be with her? It sure looked that way. And she should let herself be happy to be with him.

She switched on the radio, still on that oldies station from Friday night, and gave herself a stern talking to. *Today's your day. Don't blow it.*

When a 1980s song came on she sang along, *What*

*I like about you,* and Jack joined her as they motored through Summerland and on toward Santa Barbara. *That's what I like about you...what I like...*

She could think of a thousand things she liked about Jack. Could he come close with his list?

After the song, Jack tossed her a look. "Do you remember when the track team got to go to Magic Mountain in our junior year?"

"Of course." It had been the first chance she'd had to really spend time with Jack off campus.

"You were the only one ballsy enough to go on Dare Devil's Drop with me."

Scared out of her wits, but determined to get his attention, there was no way she would have missed that opportunity for the world. "You betcha."

He glanced at her and smiled. "That was the first time I knew you were special."

*Then why the heck hadn't he asked her out instead of her best friend?* "Really."

"Uh-huh."

Her stomach had replaced her mouth on that ride. She could only imagine how the skin on her face must have looked at G-force. Too afraid to move her head, she hadn't even glanced at Jack, barely had the chance since the ride was over almost as quickly as it had begun. She'd fought off the queasies the rest of the night, but it had been worth it just to be on a ride with Jack. And after all these years, she'd come to find out it really had been worth the terror if it had gotten Jack to take notice.

After Jack's admission, they passed self-satisfied smiles back and forth, but mostly kept quiet for the remaining miles up the coast.

"Drew keeps a small cabin cruiser docked up here." Jack tossed her a playful glance as they drove down Cabrillo Boulevard. "I've got the keys." He lifted his brows. "What do you say? Feel like a coastal cruise this afternoon?"

He could have offered a trash-collecting expedition complete with bright orange vests at this point, and still would have gotten a thumbs-up from her.

"Oh, yeah. I'd love that."

"We can grab some sandwiches and drinks and have a picnic at sea."

"Sounds great. After all the workout—" she cleared her throat and he grinned even wider "—I'm starved."

The pure happiness she witnessed on his face, coupled with a few quick flashbacks to their lovemaking sessions, put a genuine smile on her lips, too. If she kept her head on straight, she might be able to sustain it for the rest of the day. She'd just have to deal with going back to Portland later.

They parked at the docks, hiked back to the pier and caught one of the electric shuttle busses up State Street in search of food. Finding a café and sandwich shop, they placed their order and sat alfresco with coffee and a pastry to share while waiting. Though cooler in Santa Barbara, the sun was still out and there was no trace of wind.

As Anne sipped her European blend and watched

the people walk by, she felt more alive than she had in years. No more shy-girl-and-out-of-reach-jock junk. No more platonic friends. They'd finally hooked up and it was good. Damn good.

Midsip, Jack sent her a private glance filled with all the heat she could handle in public. She blew over her cup sending some of her steam his way, too. He took her hand and squeezed it, and leaned forward as if to kiss her just as their order number got called. He winked at her instead, and as he walked to the counter, she openly enjoyed the cut of his jeans thinking, I know exactly how great that looks in the buff.

The middle-aged woman at the next table noticed her lascivious grin, followed the direction of her glance and lifted her brows in understanding.

Whew, the coffee was making Anne sweat.

Jack wrapped his arm around Anne's neck while he steered the boat along the coast. For today, he felt like king of the world. The late afternoon sun changed the color of the water from minute to minute. Right now the aqua tones took a turn toward pewter blue, and a few fleecy, domed cumulus clouds hung in the sky. He kissed her temple and she hugged him tighter around the waist. Nah, it didn't get much better than this. Except for being inside her. Nothing in the world could touch that.

"You feel like eating yet?" she said.

He glanced at her with purely sexual intentions, and she cuffed his arm halfheartedly.

"You know what I mean," she said, pulling the coy girl act.

She'd been anything but when they'd had sex. Damn, she couldn't get enough of him, acted like she'd die if he didn't take her all the way, and he'd been happy to oblige. He couldn't have held out a second longer than he had. His little ol' speedy had surprised the hell out of him. He grinned for about the four-hundredth time that afternoon.

She cuffed him again. "Get your mind out of your boxers. Come on, let's eat."

"Let me pull into this cove over here first."

"Okay. I'll pour the drinks." She disappeared down into the galley.

The thirty-foot boat had a small galley and dining area, but more importantly, an aft cabin with a double-size bunk. They'd come together like a tornado that morning, both times, now Jack wanted a shot at taking his time and making love to Anne from head to toe. What better way to show her how he felt about her?

He dropped anchor and went below. She'd laid out their sandwiches and potato salad on paper plates. She'd opened a sparkling water for herself and an orange soda for him. The cozy domestic feel grabbed him around the heart and squeezed a little. This was what he'd been missing, that special ingredient, a woman—the right woman—to love. A woman he trusted and liked, and definitely had the hots for.

The sea had pinked up Anne's complexion and tossed her nutmeg-colored hair every which way, but she looked great. Her fawn brown eyes met his and he couldn't stop himself. He leaned in and kissed her long and sweet. God, he'd never get tired of those lips. Ever.

Her welcoming smile warmed him in places he'd forgotten about, like his heart and soul. It made him want to cherish and take care of her, though that could be a little tough with her living in Portland and all. He'd just have to kiss some sense into her and talk her into moving back home where everyone loved her. Was that what this was about, this heavy-lump-of-heart-in-his-chest thing? Love?

Though they ate in silence, they smiled like some of his students concealing sneaky secrets. *We had sex and it was good. When can we do it again?* He liked the carefree feel of being at sea with Anne, with just enough swell and ripple to keep things interesting.

Though he sat fantasizing more and more about what would come next, she was the one to come on to him. She'd finished her sandwich and sparkling water, wiped her mouth in a dainty fashion, belying the heat in her gaze, then walked around the tiny galley booth and sat on his lap. That smile had nothing to do with coy.

"I ought to feed you more often," he said, patting her rump and dropping a kiss on her small but ample mouth, "since it seems to make you horny."

She halfway laughed and nuzzled into his neck. Damn, that sent another message straight to his groin.

"What's wrong with a girl sitting on a guy's lap?" She lifted one pretty little brow and he about lost it right there.

"Not a thing, darlin' speedy. Did I mention this boat has a bed?" his voice sounded raspy, like a man parched for water, but in this case, sex. He needed it, thought maybe he'd die if he couldn't be with her again. Right now.

"Really."

"Uh-huh. Want to see it?"

"That's not all I want to see," she whispered.

Well that did it. They jumped on each other like they hadn't been together in a decade. They never made it to the mattress, just rocked the boat right there in the galley. And it was sweet and hot and after, as he cupped her cheeks and moved her tighter on his lap, he thought, damn, she's spoiled me for anyone else, ever again.

"You're going to have to give me a chance to take it slow with you some time."

She looked at his watch. "How about fifteen minutes from now?"

"Lord, give me strength. And another orange soda."


Jack had announced he was a man of his word on more than one occasion, and in the fading daylight of the aft cabin, he proved it to Anne. He hadn't missed one centimeter of skin from her head to her toes with his kisses, caresses, strokes and massages. He'd curled her nerve endings into oversensitive buds of anticipation, along with her toes, and if he didn't step up his game soon, she'd go crazy.

She bucked and moaned her mounting frustration.

He was a mind reader. No doubt about it. He opened

her and twirled his tongue on her most sensitive spot and only rocket science could explain the result. Sure enough, she'd have to put up with his teasing about her nickname again, and she'd love every word of it.

But nothing could compare to the deep heat when he entered her, and having taken the edge off their love-making all day, he rode her for long, luxurious, don't-ever-stop moments that coiled and tightened every cell in her body. When he made his final lunge, the force released her like a catapult over the starry horizon.

*Jack. I love you.*

"Feel like a walk on the beach?" Jack said, after they'd returned Drew's boat to the berth.

Anne's legs felt like noodles after being at sea all afternoon and evening, but the night breeze and the call of the waves crashing on the shore influenced her decision. "I'd love to."

He glanced over his shoulder at the cabin cruiser. "I'll never think the same way about that boat again."

She smiled and they passed back and forth another in their series of meaningful glances.

Anne took off her flats and pushed her jeans up her calves. The sand was cool, coarse and sticky between her toes.

He put his hands on her shoulders and pushed her toward an incoming wave. She squirmed out of his clutch and jammed him in the back, forcing his deck shoes to get wet. He chased her down the shore hollering his intentions.

"You'll be sorry!"

"You'll never catch me, Lightfoot. My nickname ain't speedy for nothin'!"

"Now I know you're delusional."

He did catch her, and flung her onto the dry sand. She kicked and protested on her way down. *Thud.*

"Jack!"

"Jack," he mocked with a girly whine.

"You did *not* just do that," she said as he laughed. "I've got sand in my jeans and…"

"I'll help you de-sand later," he said gently kissing her.

She tossed a fistful at him.

"Hey!" He sat on his heels, brushing the grainy clump from his shirt.

Only the moonbeams, the fluorescent whitecaps and the distant city provided light. She sat up. His broad silhouette hovered near with a wide white smile. Dusting his hands, he sat beside her and tossed a shell at the incoming waves. They grew quiet, and he kissed her temple.

There they sat contentedly listening to the tumble and crash and watching the tide. Her rump was cold and damp, but she wasn't ready to leave yet, especially knowing she'd fly home next weekend.

As they sat watching the sea, the negative feelings came over her like a sneaky virus. After staving off her concerns all day, maybe it was exhaustion or all the raw emotions called up by being with Jack. Whatever the reason, she'd slipped back into the old and tired song of their past, the intense history she'd been forced to relive since the moment she'd arrived home.

He glanced at her deep in thought, then did a double take. "You okay?"

She nodded, but she wasn't. Not at all.

"If I had a penny, I'd give it to you," he said.

She laid back, not caring about getting sand in her hair or down her neck or anything. She stared at the sky with only a scattering of pale stars thanks to the bright city nearby.

He came down on his elbow next to her. "What's up?"

She'd had sex with Jack four times already today. Wasn't she entitled to ask the most pressing question on her disappointingly immature, stuck-in-teen-angst mind these last twelve years?

She knew it was a stupid idiotic idea, but the dark force she'd suppressed all these years reared its head, insisting she had to know, once and for all. She took a deep breath and dove off the cliff.

"Why didn't you come after me, Jack?"

He went quiet for a moment. "I could ask the same thing, why did you leave?"

She laid still, stoic, waiting for the old scars to burst open.

"You were supposed to be my friend," he said. "It was pretty evident you didn't want me when you left."

His misinterpretation ticked her off. She sat bolt upright.

"I was sick of being your friend! That's all I'd ever

been, Jack." She grabbed and tossed a handful of sand at the ocean. "And besides, I went away to school! You knew where I was going. It wasn't like I'd dropped off the edge of the universe."

She stood and started down the beach at a brisk clip.

*Anne breathed her own stale breath under the mask. The hospital room blurred when she walked inside, but she willed herself not to cry, never to cry in front of her friend.*

*Brianna looked like a sleeping ghost, with transparent tubes running to and from her body. There was a dressing on her chest, and three lines connected to the nearby IV. Anne swallowed salty water and her hand trembled when she touched Brianna's arm. Her eyes opened slowly, and when Bri recognized Anne she smiled like an angel. She thought Bri still looked like the same girl, just a little smudged around the edges, and a tiny bit faded.*

*Her best friend was going to die. The fact knocked the air out of her with a sledgehammer of fear and sadness.*

"Are you listening to me?" Jack grabbed her arm and forced her around to face him.

*Brianna opened her eyes and faintly smiled at Anne. "Can you keep a secret?"*

*How could someone so sick still sound like a happy-go-lucky teenager?*

"You asked her to marry you," she said, with the same disbelief she'd had when Brianna had told her in the hospital.

He took a moment to compose himself.

"Yes. I promised Brianna I'd marry her, everyone knew it. How could I suddenly pick up and take off after you? Even though I'd wanted to."

She remembered Brianna's secret, how it had sliced through her heart, made her abhor Jack for being the hero he was. Made her hate herself for feeling jealous. She both despised and loved him for being a prince. And to this day, she hung her head in shame for envying her dying friend.

Anne grabbed her head. How sick and twisted was that? She wanted to cringe and scream at the same time, but the old demons wouldn't let go, she had to know.

"What would have happened if she'd lived?"

"She didn't."

"Are you saying you made empty promises to a dying woman?"

He scraped his hand through his hair and turned toward the ocean. She grabbed his arm and swung him around.

Jack's face was half covered by shadows and contorted from Anne forcing him to face the deplorable memories. "I only said the truth. What was in my heart. I ached for Bri, wished I could make her better or take her place. If a miracle happened and she went into remission, yes, I would have married her. Does that make me a horrible person?"

Tears streaked down her cheeks. "No, it makes me the most despicable person on earth for wishing you'd said something else." She took a step toward him.

"Don't you see? I still can't figure this mess out. Either I'm the worst person in the world for my feelings back then, or you're the cruelest person in the world for those empty deathbed promises." She paced around him in a circle. He stood statue still. "Either way, I can't deal with it...with us." Aware her arms were flailing—she had no control over them. "I had to leave Whispering Oaks in order to live with myself. To this day, I can't stand that I wanted my best friend's guy so much that I resented her...even when she was dying." She hugged her waist and crumbled into a heap on the sand, purging her acid memories through tears. "It doesn't get much worse than that."

"Anne, you've got to cut yourself some slack." Jack stood over her, offering a hand but she couldn't move. "We were just kids. Life isn't all black and white. I couldn't figure anything out back then, but I've had a dozen years to think it over, and I don't see either of us as villains."

He knelt beside her, and she saw the tortured expression on his face.

"I didn't want her to die," she said, her voice raspy and tired. "I swear I didn't, but live or die, either way, I'd lost you. And I'd lost her." Some new force gave her strength to get up and dust the sand from her clothes. She stuck out her chin. "And you know what? If she'd lived, I would have been her maid of honor and never let on how I felt." She wiped her cheeks, dug in her jacket pocket for a tissue and blew her nose. "I had to leave after you proposed to her, Jack. It was my only choice."

He took her by her arms and held her firm, staring her down. "After what happened back at my house and on that boat, I've got three words for you—get over it! It's long overdue, and if I mean one damned thing to you, you're gonna have to leave all of that behind for good." He gave her a minishake. "I don't want it messing with us. Do you hear me?"

She slumped against his tightening grip. "I'm sorry, Jack, but I don't think I can...."

They stared at each other, their final showdown. Jack was the first to break away. He paced back and forth a few times, searching the sky, grabbing his hair. "What about today?"

Her chin trembled but she forced her words out steady. "We had a good time. That's all." The last phrase trickled on a whisper.

He shook his head. "You lie."

Yes, she was lying, but somehow it seemed the only way she could survive right now. "We had sex. People do it all the time."

He stared at her as if she'd escaped the mental ward. His expression soon changed to one of understanding, and he was on to her and her ridiculous circle-of-life question about why he'd never come after her. And then, changing again, he looked super pissed off that she'd forced an answer out of him.

"You think I don't get that sex with you means something? Guys don't tread near women like you unless they're serious." He moved closer. She almost flinched. "Sex with you meant we'd be a couple, Anne. That's how I've always seen it. I wasn't ready for forever back then in high school. Or right after graduation. I couldn't come after you. But I'm here now."

"You said I was the one, Jack. Then a couple months later you asked Bri to marry you, but I held on to those words. I thought, maybe he'll remember what he said, and I waited my entire first year in college for you. Then I heard you were traveling, so I waited the second year."

She dared to glance into his face. Dark, angry angles stared out at her from the shadows. "After the fourth year, I quit waiting," she said, hardly audible over the waves.

Feeling like a stubborn child, she toed the sand, assured in her status as the queen of ruining a perfect day.

"Are you saying it's too late?" Jack stared out to sea, his voice husky in the night air.

"I'm saying I don't know anymore," she said, resigned, defeated, exhausted.

He stepped in front of her. She suffered through another stone-cold angry stare down, but willed herself through it. Willed her eyes to stay steady. Willed back her threatening tears. "I guess we should go," she whispered on a quivery breath.

He followed her toward the car, opened the door for her and watched her get inside.

"For your information," he said, "this wasn't a date. This was us finally getting it together."

*And me, tearing everything apart.*

Chewing her bottom lip, stuck in her sorry rut because she'd already ruined everything so why bother to say another word, she remained silent and let that be her final answer.

"Then I guess that's that, isn't it." He closed the door and strode around to his side and got in.

They drove the entire distance home without another word.

## Chapter Ten

Anne let herself out of Jack's car without saying a word and headed for her front door. He sat stoically behind the wheel, didn't even glance her way. Dizzy with remorse, and her stomach so tight she thought she might puke, she strode on. Jack backed out of the driveway, shifted to Drive, peeled rubber and sped down the street as if a drag car racer, or a hotheaded teen.

A gust of wind hit her in the face like a rude wake-up call. Their renewed relationship had ended before it even got started. Because of her and her inability to let go of the past. She took a quivery breath and tightened her knees. The last thing she wanted to do was face her family in this state.

She stood on the porch, took several more breaths, deeper and deeper, and shook her head, trying to get rid of the nightmare that had just occurred. *Get it to-gether, Anne. Don't let them see you like this.* Her mother would be on to her in a flash if she saw how shell-shocked she was. One more breath, a quick throat clearing and eye swipe and she put her key into the lock, willing her roiling feelings to settle down, to play nice and pretend everything was right as the wind in Whispering Oaks.

Opening the front door, she stepped inside to a heated game of video tennis in the family room. Thank-fully, Mom, Dad and Lucas were all distracted by the tournament. Bart lifted his head from his paws and quickly went back to the nap on his bed, too lazy to walk over and give her a hello sniff.

"Hey, look at this, Annie belle, I can beat your brother at tennis with one hand!" He waved the hand-held gizmo that controlled the racket and ball on the TV.

She wanted to scream and run down the hall to her bedroom, slam the door and face-plant on her bed, but she had to keep it together. Just a few more moments. "That's great, Dad."

*Thwap.* Lucas made a serve so strong it knocked Kieran's avatar on its backside. The game flashed on applause in the grandstands as if in Wimbledon, with funny little round heads bobbing and swaying.

Kieran gave Lucas a suspecting stare, one brow arched. "Been holding back, eh?"

Lucas shrugged the exact way he used to when he was a kid and Dad routinely underestimated him. The almost unnoticeable twitch at the corner of his mouth had always been his tell. She saw it now. He'd been letting Dad win.

Under normal circumstances, this would have made her laugh, but she'd numbed herself in order to face her family. Hanging on to her facade by a thread, she continued on toward the kitchen, rather than run directly to her room, which is what she really wanted to do.

Her mother's laser stare followed Anne as she went for a drink of water. She didn't need to see it to feel it. She held the glass with a trembling hand, drank and prayed she could make it down the hall without having to answer any questions.

"How was your day?" her mother's voice came from behind.

She swung around. "Oh. It was nice. We had a good time. Thanks." She put the glass on the counter so her mother couldn't see her shaking. "But I'm exhausted and think I'll go to bed now."

Her mother stood her ground and stared, concern pinching her brows. "That's it? You only had a good time?"

Anne had to distract her.

"Yep. Hey, shouldn't you get to bed early, too, since you start teaching tomorrow?"

"It's only 10:00." Beverly's suspicious expression had Anne nearly speed walking for the hall.

"Well, I'm exhausted. See you in the morning."

"Match point!" Kieran called out from the couch,

lifting his good arm as if he'd just taken one giant step for mankind.

Anne yawned as she passed through the family room. "Night all." Hopefully no one picked up on the waver in her voice.

The last thing she wanted to do was rehash with her mother the ongoing, most confusing and biggest mess of her life. Jack. How could doing what your gut thought was right, feel so wrong? And now that she'd said she could never "get over it" aloud, to Jack, she couldn't take it back. He knew she was a lost cause.

Jack pushed the speed limit, but hit every streetlight. Just his luck.

That's what he got for telling a woman how he felt—*Today was about us finally getting it together*—a door slammed firmly in his face.

Except he hadn't said the actual words *I love you and want to be with you.* For all Anne knew, he just wanted to have sex with her. Couldn't she tell that he loved her? And judging by the way she'd totally given herself to him, he'd thought that maybe, just maybe, she loved him, too.

Then what the hell happened?

How could things have gotten any more screwed up?

If Brianna hadn't gotten sick, he would have broken up with her for Anne. And yeah, the truth wasn't always pretty. Life sure as hell had a surprise in store for all of them. Poor Bri. God, it hurt to watch her get sicker and sicker, to see her suffer, so he proposed. *All he wanted to do was ease her pain, give her hope, offer something to live for. Was being a bride enough to make her keep fighting the losing battle?* Not that he was the greatest catch in the world, but long before she'd gotten leukemia she'd said she loved him—when she sensed he was cooling off to her, and that maybe there was someone else. He'd made sure she never had any idea that the other "someone" had been Anne.

Truth was, if she'd survived, he would have kept his word and married her. Keeping on that truth trail, they both would have been miserable, and wasn't he a damn heel for thinking it. That bit of honesty had sometimes made it hard to look at himself in the mirror, but it would only have been a matter of time before they'd broken up. That, without a doubt, would have been inevitable.

Jack scraped fingers through his hair, fighting off a wave of panic.

Tonight he'd given Anne an ultimatum—*get over it*—and she'd said she couldn't.

So that was that then. Years and years of waiting for the right time, a chance to spend time with her, a day of great sex and companionship, followed by the realization they could never be together.

Life sucked.

He bashed the wheel with his palm. What a freaking huge disappointment Anne had turned out to be.

Jack parked in his garage, feeling queasy from all the drama. He hadn't let anyone make him physically sick since his mother had left or when Brianna had died. Anne wasn't supposed to belong to that notorious group.

*Yeah? Well, think again, buddy. Turns out life is full of junk that wasn't supposed to happen. It's just the way it is.*

He slammed the car door and went inside. How in the hell was he going to sleep in the same bed they'd burned up with hot sex just that morning?

He stood still for a moment.

Well, wasn't that what the guest room was for?

The next morning, though she'd hardly slept a wink, Anne got up early to help her mother prepare for her first day back at school. She blow-dried and combed out Beverly's hair and helped her put on some mascara, all the while hoping her mom wouldn't give her the third degree.

"You seemed a little upset last night," Beverly said, while Anne sprayed her hair.

So much for hope. "I was just tired." Short. Clipped.

"I don't believe you for one minute. I'm your mother, remember?" Beverly glanced over her shoulder at her.

Anne couldn't meet her eyes. "Mom we had a great time." *If you don't count the meltdown on the beach.* "He took me for breakfast. We drove up the coast and enjoyed the sunshine. We went for a boat ride around the shore. We had a late lunch, walked on the beach and came home." All said with a lack of one important ingredient—enthusiasm.

"Why do I get the distinct impression you're not telling me the whole story."

Anne sighed. "Mom, I'd rather not talk about it." *Because it's none of your business and I haven't begun to figure anything out.* "Here." She held up a hand mirror for her mother's inspection.

"Looks good, but I don't know why I bothered with it. Did you hear the wind last night?"

"How could I not?" The house creaked and strained under the constant assault of what felt like fifty-mile-an-hour wind, wind that dried and singed everything in its path. She glanced through the kitchen window at the brittle brown grass on the hill behind their house. It looked the same way her heart felt, all dried out.

Beverly held the mirror with her one good hand. "My bangs. See right there?"

Anne gave a look then nodded.

"Can you plump them up?"

She used a wide-toothed pick to lift the bangs and primp the crown of her mother's layered cut. After a month of styling Mom's hair, Anne knew exactly what she wanted.

"There. Thanks." Beverly stood. "Lucky for you I'm distracted about going back to school and my class, otherwise, I'd grill you more about your date yesterday."

Anne said a little prayer of thanks.

"Well, there's always tonight." Beverly put the mirror on the kitchen table, lifted her brow at Anne then started for the other room. "I always thought Jack was the perfect guy for you and, well, I'd hate to think I was wrong."

"Get dressed, Mom, or you'll be late." *You were wrong. I was wrong. The whole Jack thing was wrong. From the beginning!* She had as much acid in her stomach as if she'd drunk the entire pot of coffee by herself.

"You're driving me, right?"

"Yes." Anne stared straight ahead rather than look at her mother. "Call me when you're ready."

As soon as Mom disappeared, she strode to her room, closed and leaned against the door, and did something she hadn't allowed since last night. She wept. Silently. She wrapped her arms around her waist, bent over and opened her mouth, letting out soft sputters and odd clicking sounds from the back of her throat. Quiet enough so no one could hear her pain.

"Drew? It's Jack." He called his best friend just before he left to drive to school Monday morning. "Hey, can I take out one of your hot air balloons this weekend?"

Sleeping in the guest room—actually, *not* sleeping *while* in the guest room—had forced Jack to think all night. The ultimatum he'd given Anne may have backfired, but he wasn't ready to give up. As simple as it seemed, he'd come up with a last-ditch plan to win her back.

"If these winds keep up, it might not be safe."

"You've got a point," Jack said. "Let's hope for better

weather." And while he was at it, he'd hope that Anne would hear him out.

"Sure, man. Anytime you want to fly, weather permitting, a balloon is yours."

He'd give Anne a couple days to come to her senses, then he'd try again. He wouldn't give up this time, wouldn't let her slip away, but confronting her now would be pointless. Yeah, he'd give her a day or two to cool off, talk to her on Wednesday after he drove Kieran to his doctor's appointment. He'd ask her to take another ride in the sky then he'd tell her how he really felt.

If she knew that he'd loved her since the day he'd told her that she was the one, well, just maybe she'd forgive him for taking so long to get around to doing anything about it. And if he was lucky, she'd finally leave Bri out of the equation and start fresh with him. Just the two of them.

The thing was, he had to tell her. She needed to hear him say it.

Anne drove through the circular driveway of her old grammar school, stopped, hopped out and ran around the other side to open the door for her mother. Was this how it had felt dropping her brother, sister and her off at school all those years ago? Compelled to hand her mother a lunch box and kiss her cheek, Anne stopped short.

"Here you go. I made it myself." It was a brown bag

lunch with a sparkling lime drink and a chicken salad sandwich on seven grain bread. Her mother's favorite.

"Thanks, kid. Wish me luck."

"You don't need it, Mom, you're a natural-born teacher."

"Mrs. Grady! Mrs. Grady!" A group of anxiously waving ten-year-old girls called out from the nearby grass. "Can we see your cast?"

Beverly glanced at Anne and winked as a gust of wind wreaked havoc with her carefully combed hair. "It's showtime."

Anne got back into the car and watched her mother enter the school surrounded by adoring students, and for the first time that day, she smiled.

After making a grocery run, she returned home to find her father and brother behind closed bathroom doors. From the sound of it, Kieran was getting a birdbath.

She took the opportunity to boot up the family computer and check out one-way flights for Portland.

Before she did, though, she remembered the website Jack had told her about, the one for the RN-to-M.D.-friendly programs. His consideration still touched her heart. She made a quick visit and bookmarked it for future browsing, then shook her head. She couldn't deny Jack cared for her. He'd shown it in so many ways over the past month. Hell, right about now she could use a long Rollerblade ride down her street, and with this wind she wouldn't even need to skate! How much did the man have to do to prove to her how he felt?

Refusing to get distracted because she had a job and a boss waiting for her, but mostly because her brain ached from all the unanswered questions marching through her head, she got back on task and brought up the airline website. And a few moments later found the flight.

Saturday, 10:00 a.m. from LAX to Portland, arrival 2:15 p.m. Without a second thought, she got out her credit card and booked a seat.

"What're you up to?" Lucas asked.

"I just bought my ticket home for Saturday. You'll be fine on your own with Mom and Dad, won't you?"

"Sure. Hey, did you buy any peanut butter?"

"Yeah, but you have to stir it first." She noticed Bart had been warming up to Lucas and was hot on his heels right now. She followed both of them into the kitchen.

"Where's Dad?"

"Still in the bathroom. There are some things a man needs to do all by himself."

"You've got a point."

Lucas washed his hands and opened the jar, stirred the peanut butter then jammed a spoon inside and ate it straight. Bart sat at his feet salivating. When Lucas had finished he let Bart lick what was left as he scratched the dog's ears.

"Lucas!" Kieran bellowed.

"Well, my fifteen-minute union break is up." Lucas tossed the spoon into the sink and took off down the hall. Bart ran after him.

With Lucas home picking up the biggest share of the

load, and having run out of things to do, Anne couldn't avoid thinking of Jack. Honestly, she'd never stopped.

She'd have to see him Wednesday when he drove Kieran to his doctor's appointment. What would she say? Would she be able to look him in the face? The mere thought made her stomach as tight as a twine ball.

He'd asked her to get over it. To get over the fact he'd asked Bri to marry him when she was dying. He had no idea how devastating it had been, how many years she'd worked to forget it, to move on. And she finally had. Coming home and spending time with Jack had brought everything back, as if it had all happened yesterday. Thousands of feelings blew through her faster than the current wind in Whispering Oaks.

Truth was, there were some events in life she couldn't get past, and she just had to learn to live with it. So far, since she'd been home, she hadn't been able to "get over it" as Jack had so succinctly put it. He'd acted like a prince back then, and she'd been kicked to the sidelines, a place she'd gotten sick of being where Bri and Jack were concerned.

He'd hurt her more than he could ever know, and would have to live with the consequences.

She bit her bottom lip and shook her head. She'd have to live with those damned consequences, too.


Anne picked up her mother from school and got an ear load about the first day back.

"I'm exhausted. Even with the teacher's aide, I never

sat down. Look." She thrust out her casted arm. "They all wanted to sign it. Isn't that sweet?"

Despite looking near haggard, Beverly hadn't been this animated since Anne had arrived in town. In her mixed up and near crazy-with-doubt mind, Anne found the distraction to be pure joy.

"Even that Ricky Milligan kid?"

Beverly batted her lashes. "He was a perfect angel. Though I'm not holding my breath on how he'll behave tomorrow."

They smiled at each other. Anne didn't want to burst her mother's bubble of happiness, so she held off on telling her that she'd be leaving on Saturday.

"Annie belle, could you throw another shrimp on the barbie?" Kieran said. "I invited Jocelyn for dinner." He'd parked his wheelchair by the opened garage, where Lucas tinkered on the old Mustang. Since he'd broken his arm, he was no longer able to use crutches.

She'd just finished grilling a platter full of veggies on the built-in patio barbecue pit. "I can do that."

Before she went inside, she watched her father cast a melancholy glance toward his totaled Harley parked at the side of the garage.

Her mother sat at the kitchen table going over a pile of school papers, and Anne had another flash of role reversal. The eerie feeling gave her chills. *I really need to get home and take back my life.*

"Anne? Can you write *excellent* across the top of this paper?"

Her mother was grading spelling tests, perfectly able to make *X*s with her left hand, but still not able to write comments.

"Don't you have stickers for that?"

"Yeah, but some of the fourth grade kids think they're too grown-up for stickers. This precocious girl is one of them."

"Ha! I *still* like stickers."

"Yes, dear, but you're special." Her mother gave her a goofy grin.

Anne shook her head. "Tell you what, I'm busy cooking dinner now, but how about you grade the tests and I'll sit with you later and write anything you want on them. Or, you could ask Dad. He's still got his one good hand."

Beverly gave an incredulous look. "Have you tried to read your father's writing lately?"

"Good point." Even deciphering doctors' orders had been easier than decoding her father's handwriting.

"Oh, look at this, Ricky Milligan got 100%! Maybe I should have broken my arm at the beginning of the semester."

Anne smiled to herself as she walked back to the kitchen counter. She basted the super large shrimp with olive oil, lemon juice and seasoning and carried them outside to start grilling just as Jocelyn rounded the patio corner. She didn't want to make a big deal out of it, but it was quite obvious her neighbor had dolled herself up.

"You look cute," Anne said. "What's the occasion?"

Jocelyn did a quick flash of her attire, cropped pants,

double-layered formfitting tank tops, adorable sandals and fresh pedicure. "I came straight from school. Anything I can do?"

"I've got it covered. Why don't you go say hi to Dad and Lucas."

Jocelyn looked dumbstruck momentarily, but recovered quickly. It would be the first time she'd seen Lucas since he'd come home. She headed toward the garage just as Lucas came outside.

"Hey," he said with a hint of surprise in his eyes which, in Anne's opinion, he totally underplayed. Typical of him.

"Hi, Lucas." Her step faltered, but Anne was quite sure only she'd noticed.

Jocelyn opened her arms. Lucas gave her a one-armed quickie hug, which looked more out of obligation than sincere. Even Anne felt disappointed. An awkward moment followed when Jocelyn wasn't sure what to do with her hands so she shoved them in her back pockets, and another when she looked into his eyes and he evaded her gaze.

"How are you?" she asked.

"Fine. Just fine." He glanced at the ground. "I hear you're house-sitting for your parents."

"Yeah, they're finally taking that road trip they've always dreamed about."

"There she is," Kieran said, rolling out of the garage.

"You wanted to talk to me, Coach Grady?"

Lucas chuckled. "Oh, yeah, he's got big plans for track this season. How are you with micromanaging?"

"I'm right here and I can hear you," Dad said.

Lucas gave Jocelyn a warning glance. "Let me know if you need backup."

"That's the last time I run my game plan by you." No one, not even Anne, believed Dad's threat. The man couldn't keep his thoughts to himself if he duct taped his mouth.

"I guess I'd better see what you've got in mind." Jocelyn stepped behind the wheelchair and rolled it toward the back door with the makeshift ramp. Over her shoulder, she mouthed thanks to Lucas.

"Good luck," he called out.

She blushed and smiled.

"Don't listen to him, Jocelyn," Kieran said.

Lucas watched Jocelyn as she pushed Kieran into the house. Yeah, big sisters noticed things like that, even when they were supposed to be barbecuing shrimp.

Once her father and Jocelyn were out of earshot, Anne whispered like a kid on the playground. "She is so adorable, don't you think?"

"Back off, sis," he said as he headed toward the garage. "Dad's already taken it on to play matchmaker, whether I want him to or not. I don't need you doing it, too."

Matchmaker?

Dear God, she really was turning into her mother.


Tuesday morning Jack sat in the teacher's lounge before first period drinking his coffee. If he had another night without sleep, he'd have to mainline caffeine in order to stay awake in school.

Jocelyn rushed through the door, hair blown every which way, school papers practically flying from her folder. "I didn't think it could get any worse. It's like a hurricane without the rain out there."

Jack nodded. "It's pretty bad, all right."

"I'll have to cancel track practice today," she said.

He'd already received a call to come directly to the fire department after school. A small brushfire had started in Wind Canyon, the wind had taken care of the rest. Even as Jack drank his coffee, firemen were fighting to save a house in the cul-de-sac at the base of the canyon.

"I had dinner with the Gradys last night," she said, plopping her things on a table.

Great, just what he needed to be reminded of, the Gradys and their stubborn-to-a-fault daughter.

"Lucas looks great, but really tired. Hey, did you know Anne's leaving for home this Saturday?" she said, reorganizing her papers.

Jack almost choked on his coffee. Anne was leaving? That was it? She was just going to turn tail and get out of town without talking to him again?

Disappointment cut so deep he found it hard to breathe.

## Chapter Eleven

Lucas woke up Kieran extra early on Wednesday morning to help him get ready for his appointment. Anne assisted her mother as she prepared for her third day back at work. It felt oddly like the hustle and bustle of the good old days, except without Lark, when the entire family rushed to get ready for school. It made her miss her sister and wonder how she was doing, and she decided to call her later to let her know she was going home on the weekend.

If Anne planned it right, she and Mom would leave the house before Jack arrived to pick up her Dad. According to Kieran he'd once again gone above and beyond the call by taking the morning off in order to drive him in the van to the doctor. Lucas planned to accompany Dad, which left Anne off the hook. For now.

She knew she couldn't leave town without facing him again, though what in the world she planned to say was anyone's guess. *You're the lover I've always dreamed about. Goodbye?* Or, *no one has ever looked out for me the way you do. Thanks for the med school info, and I'll look you up the next time I'm in town?* She needed to gather her thoughts and seriously get it together before she saw Jack again. Until then, she'd stay out of his path.

Kieran used the automatic forward button on the wheelchair to roll himself down the hall and into the kitchen. Lucas must have been getting dressed, now that he'd dressed Dad.

"Annie belle, we'll never make it there on time with the rush-hour traffic if we don't leave soon," Kieran said, brows bunched. "It's not like Jack to be late."

She knew how anxious he was to hear how soon the leg cast could come off and how much longer he'd have to wear the one on his arm. She couldn't wait to find out, either. Being sedentary was taking its toll on Kieran, making him grumpy and restless. Not to mention missing his track team. The man should be wearing a ball cap and blowing a whistle, timing events and hollering encouragement as his runners sped by, not lounging around in a fancy electric wheelchair with a special leg extension and an extra wide armrest, on loan from their medical insurance company.

Just last night, he'd mentioned he'd even missed his remedial math students, which proved he was definitely going stir-crazy.

"Give Jack a call." She tried to sound casual, and hoped he wouldn't ask her to do it.

"I already did. It went right to his voice mail."

"Maybe he's on his way, then. You know it's against the law to talk on the cell phone while driving." She pretended to be distracted with getting her mother's lunch out of the refrigerator. All the while, she fought off the panicky feeling rising in her stomach over the possibility of seeing Jack.

"Good point, but maybe I need a plan B."

Anne tuned out as her father fiddled with his cell phone, Bart thinking it was a game and trying to pry it out of his hand. "Leave it. Leave it! Sit."

She rushed into the pantry to grab more bottled water for the refrigerator. She still wasn't ready to face Jack, to see the disappointment in his eyes again. To sense how she'd let both of them down with her inability to let go of the past. Here she thought she was a modern day woman, but somehow by coming home again, the old pain and insecurities still held her hostage. She'd always think of herself as second best with Jack. Stupid? Yes. Amendable? Only time would tell, and who had time when she was leaving on Saturday? And all the more reason to get out of town. Instead of grabbing life by the horns, she'd been huddling in the shadows pretending to be alive, never really connecting with any man since Jack. What a disappointment she'd turned out to be.

She backed out of the pantry. "Are you ready, Ma?"

"Just about." Beverly rushed into the kitchen. "Let me say goodbye to your dad, and then we can go."

Kieran had drifted back into the other room, found Bart's favorite squeaky tennis ball and traded it for the cell. Beverly crossed into the family room, bent over Kieran and kissed him as if he were a five-year-old. "I'll call you at recess to find out how the appointment went." He pulled her back and gave her a proper kiss. All the way in the kitchen, Anne could see a spark in his eyes and had to look away.

That spark was the look of a man thoroughly in love with his woman. She'd seen it before...in Jack's eyes.

"Let's go, Mom. I'll get the car."

She headed for the garage, only then noticing the strange orange cast of the sky and the distinct smell of smoke. She stopped and glanced around, as a gust of wind blew over her. Fine ash fell like dirty snow. In the distance, behind the brown rolling foothills, out beyond Boulder Peak, several plumes of dark smoke rose and polluted the sky.

She'd been so wrapped up in her personal crisis that she'd tuned out the world. Somewhere in Whispering Oaks, the hills and canyons were on fire. Old memories of wildfires burning a path through neighboring streets fifteen years earlier sent a chill up her back. They'd been packed and ready to evacuate, but the gales had died down and the order to leave never came. If the wind continued as it was, it would be impossible to stop the dangerous flames, and who knew how much devastation it would wreak. Anne stood still, watching the sky and prayed the wind would stop.

Once she got into the car she flipped on the radio and tuned to a local station. The news was grim. Several hundred acres had already burned. A half-dozen houses in one of the canyons had been destroyed, another dozen threatened. Fortunately, there'd been no loss of life. Yet.

Anne backed out the car and helped her mother inside. She recognized the concerned expression on her face. She'd seen it every year growing up, during fire season.

"We'll have to keep the kids inside for recess and lunch today. The air is too unhealthy."

At school, the principal, some teachers and the yard duty ladies were meeting the kids at the curb and whisking them inside to the auditorium/cafeteria to wait until the bell rang. The students seemed wild-eyed and excited, like corralled colts during a lightning storm.

"Call me if you need me," she said to her mother.

"The fire looks really far away. We should be all right." The words were meant to be reassuring, but her mother's tense eyes and creased brow told another tale.

On the drive home, Anne had to take a detour since Titan Canyon Road had been blocked off by the police. She slowed down when she went by, glancing at the long road which twisted and turned into the back hills. A bright red fire truck from Los Angeles howled through the intersection and waited for the police to open the barricade to let them pass. The mobile command must be somewhere down in there.

As she drove home, she watched through the rearview mirror and saw the mushroom cloud of billowing smoke several hills over. In between that hill and her street the dried, hay-colored foothills stood helpless and ready to ignite. It would only take a spark traveling on a wind gust. The thought made her shudder.

When Anne finally arrived home, Lucas and Kieran were gone.

At least she'd avoided Jack, but she still felt like hell, and the fire fueled the raging acid in her stomach.

It hadn't rained since Christmas, and the fluke Santa Ana–styled gales had arrived extra early this year. If history repeated itself—and in Whispering Oaks, history always repeated itself—the fire would rage by afternoon.

Jack had been up all night fighting back wildfire. The furious sound of inferno hot fire deafened him.

If they didn't prevent it from burning farther back into the canyon, they'd be faced with crown fires on top of everything else.

How much more could his crew deal with?

Stretched to the limit, he worked on a twenty-person crew building a firebreak around the eastern perimeter in hopes of keeping it from spreading to the oak groves.

Jack bent, noting the ache in his tired and overused back, and pushed more debris out of the way with his shovel, tedious, but necessary work. Even now, he couldn't get the thought of losing Anne out of his mind.

Through the living room window, Anne watched a red SUV pull into the driveway. She squinted and saw her brother in the passenger seat and, was it Jocelyn driving?

She rushed out the kitchen door to greet them. "Whose car is this?"

"Jocelyn borrowed her boyfriend's car," Lucas said.

"Ex-boyfriend," Jocelyn corrected from behind the steering wheel.

"Jack never showed," Lucas said, stating the obvious, as he helped Kieran get into the waiting wheelchair.

"Yeah, I figured that out," Anne said, unable to ignore her disappointment.

"He was called in yesterday after school when the fire first started," Jocelyn said.

Anne's heart stumbled over the next couple beats, realizing where Jack was and why he wasn't here. She'd been selfishly thinking he'd wanted to avoid her as much as she did him, but that wasn't Jack's style and this proved it.

As worry took hold, Anne tried to distract herself. "How'd the appointment go?"

"Wow. Look at that smoke," Kieran said. "I hope the wind doesn't turn and bring it this way."

"Dad's leg is coming along fine," Lucas answered for him. "Two more weeks with the cast, then physical therapy and a brace. A couple weeks after that, he should get the arm cast off, and they'll discuss removing the hardware in the arm down the road."

"Over my dead body," Kieran said. "I am not going through another surgery."

"Maybe you won't have to, Dad," Anne said. "Think positive." Since when had she become the purveyor of positive thinking?

Anne walked around to the driver's side to Jocelyn. "Did Jack say anything about how they'd use their volunteer guys?"

Jocelyn rolled down the window and gazed at Anne. "He's had the same training as the regular firemen. He's probably on the front line like everyone else."

Fear balled into a lump in Anne's stomach. The thought of Jack walking into the flames...well, she couldn't let herself think about it. Yet, she couldn't *not* think about it, either. He could get injured or, worse yet...

Jocelyn must have noticed her concern. She patted her hand. "He'll be okay, Anne. He knows what he's doing."

"I hope to God you're right." The alternative made her hands tremble. What if she never got to see him again?

*Anne shifted on Jack's lap. Her breasts pressed against his chest. His hands followed the satin soft skin along the hourglass shape of her back, waist and hips. He pulled her closer. Her plump lips pressed to his as she bucked over him.*

"Jack!"

His eyes popped open on an inhale. "Yeah," he said, husky voiced.

"Grab your equipment. Let's go."

His unit had been given a short break at the command post. He'd quickly fallen asleep…and had a dream about Anne. What else was new? He rubbed his eyes hoping to wake up a little more. He hopped on the back of an old hay wagon on loan from a nearby farmer, and rode with his unit out to the mouth of the next canyon.

As predicted, the fire had jumped to the century-old oaks and their job was to save as many as they could and to keep the fire from going any farther back.

Exhausted and beat up from fighting the fire for over twenty-four hours, he sat on the flatbed with the others, in silence, watching the looming flames through the smoke, wondering how in the hell they'd tame that beast. None of the crew had much to say as dusk turned the distant orange sunset to a magnificent red. In the direction they headed, the sky was hidden behind a curtain of black and gray smoke. Behind them, charred earth and rock with tree skeletons still smoking, as desolate as the moon. He'd never get the picture out of his mind or the stench out of his nose.

Throughout all of this, one thought played over and over in his mind. Anne will be leaving. He'd lived without her all these years, but losing her after finally making love with her made him queasy. Sure, he could make it through life alone; he'd been doing an adequate job so far. But life would be a hell of a lot sweeter, especially after a day and night like this, knowing someone waited and worried for him. Someone like her, exactly like Anne.

The wagon came to a stop several hundred feet back from a long line of yellow and red fire trucks. They all jumped off and collected their gear. Heat from the fire rim hit him like a hot hair dryer in his face. He put on his helmet, flash hood and visor and followed the group to the frontline fire hoses. Overhead another fire tanker chopped through the air dropping its load along the periphery.

"We're moving in down here," his unit leader yelled, gesturing in the direction.

Jack grabbed onto the water hose and pulled with the others as they all followed.

Whirling heat raged in the near distance. It had jumped the fire break they'd cleared yesterday. Their hoses seemed futile to fight the demon flames, but they trudged on. Radiant heat felt like a baking oven through his personal protective gear, but he moved onward with his unit.

In the midst of hell on earth, fighting back the fire, trying to save the next acre of land, he realized some things were worth fighting for. Like his hometown, and those he loved.

Anne was a woman worth fighting for and, the moment he got the chance, he'd be at her door, insisting she hear him out. This time he wouldn't take her silence as an answer. He'd force her to talk it out, to explain to him how they could make love the way they had and not be crazy about each other. He knew without a doubt he loved her. Always had.

A gust of wind howled through the canyon. Heat, like a beach wave, made Jack lose his balance. He adjusted his stance to stabilize. Overhead oak crowns burned bright and quickly like huge flaming flowers. Smoke and fire whirled through the trees in a crazy dance. They moved closer with their hoses full blast, yet only licking at the flames. A futile exercise.

And still they pushed forward.

"Get out! Get out!" The muffled words came from behind along with a loud crack.

Jack held tight to the hose and back-stepped. Pain exploded through his shoulder, forcing the air from his lungs as he got knocked to the ground.

## Chapter Twelve

Anne couldn't sleep knowing Jack was out there risking his life fighting the fires. She lay in Lark's old twin bed staring at the ceiling, ignoring the stupid unicorns circling the walls. Her parents had never redecorated the room, which made it feel like a time capsule.

Flipping onto her side, she punched her pillow, dug her head into it and fussed until she got comfortable. That lasted five seconds. Finally giving up, she threw back the blanket, sat up and turned on the light, soon pacing the length of the room, stubbing her toe on the Rollerblades Jack had loaned her. She could use a soothing roll down the hill right about now, but the smoke would ruin everything. And there she was back to thinking about Jack again. She doubted she'd ever be able to forget him.

Her parents had stored lots of junk from her old room in here, along with her sister's. Having ruled out skating, she opened the closet and looked at the row of high school yearbooks on the upper shelf. She'd been purposely avoiding them since she'd first arrived. Being home had been catalyst enough when it came to bad memories.

Against her better judgment, she reached for her senior yearbook with the Whispering Oaks mascot on the cover. Otis Oak Tree. God, could it have been any more lame?

Resisting the urge to open the damn book, she clutched it to her chest and went back to pacing.

Midstep, she stopped short to listen to a new sound. The sound of silence.

The wind had stopped.

She cracked open the door and tiptoed down the hall to the family room and peered through the sliding glass doors outside. The trees weren't swaying. The chimes weren't tinkling. The wind *had* stopped.

The light was on in the garage again, and she wondered if Lucas ever slept.

Anne slid open the patio door and stepped into the night. Calm and quiet welcomed her. The restless gusts had passed onward to new territory leaving debris and destruction in their path. She inhaled dormant, smoke-scented air. Glancing from the leaf-strewn yard, she could see a line of fire sitting like a flaming crown on a distant hill.

Jack was there.

Her chest squeezed thinking about him.

She continued on to the garage, where Lucas repeated his nightly ritual of tinkering with his beloved car in place of sleeping.

He glanced up. "Hey." She could hear vintage rock music playing softly in the background on an ancient static-ridden radio.

"I couldn't sleep. I'm worried about Jack."

He nodded. "At least the wind has stopped. That should give the firemen a break."

"Yeah." She traced the outline of the primer-colored car with her finger, opened the door and sat inside, putting the yearbook in the other bucket seat. "What color are you going to paint this?"

"Vintage skylight blue. What else?"

She laughed. "Isn't that a girlie color?"

He glared at her. "It's classic 1964 Mustang. And there's nothing *girlie* about a Mustang."

She placed her hands on the steering wheel, the feel of it bringing back a pocketful of memories, and she grew serious. "Do you remember when I found out you'd started smoking and I showed you a picture of the inside of a dead guy's lungs from my anatomy book?"

He lifted his head and quirked an eyebrow. "How could I forget."

"Yeah, and I blackmailed you into joining the track team with me?"

"Yes, you did." He pointed the wrench at her and tapped the air. "You still owe me for that."

She smiled. "Get off it. You were great at track. Anyway, I did it so I could meet Jack Lightfoot."

"You think I didn't know that?"

"Was I that transparent?"

He stopped tinkering, nailed her with a stare then rolled his eyes.

"Okay, so I wasn't subtle. Anyway, you know the rest of the story, but I never told anyone that Jack had kissed me once. Twice, actually." He'd kissed her a whole lot more since then, and done some amazing things to her body, too, but there were some conversations a girl didn't share with her brother. "He was going to break up with Brianna...for *me.* Then she got sick and everything else didn't matter, and we never talked about it again."

Lucas seemed to be intent on whatever he was working on, but Anne could tell she had his attention.

"And remember when Mom and Dad broke the news to me that I couldn't be premed because they couldn't afford to take out loans?"

He nodded.

"You snuck me one of Mom's wine coolers, the kind that tasted like raspberry soda, and I sat right here and drank it. Then when I was feeling tipsy, I confessed that I loved Jack, and I made you promise never to tell anyone."

"I didn't, either."

"I knew I could trust you."

He smiled at her, and for a glimpse she saw her kid brother, the smart and mischievous outsider, the person he used to be before he went away and came back so cautious and distant. She missed that guy.

"Remember the night before I left for college, when I came and sat here and told you that I still loved Jackson Lightfoot but I could never have him?"

Lucas screwed up his face. "Uh, kinda."

Anne tossed back her head. "Damn, Lucas, I break open my heart and spill my guts to you and you don't remember?"

"I didn't say I didn't remember. I just said it's a little vague. Why don't you run it by me again?" He picked up a wrench and tightened something in the belly of the car—at least that was what it looked like to her since she knew squat about cars.

"I sat right here and told you how we'd met at a coffee shop that afternoon. How I'd accused him of being stuck in a rut in Whispering Oaks. How I was hoping he'd see my point and move to Oregon where I'd be." She sighed, but it didn't come close to relieving the heaviness in her chest. "It didn't work out the way I'd planned, he'd just stared at me and told me that moving away didn't equal moving forward."

"Oh, yeah. He made a good point there."

"You're supposed to be on my side, and honestly I didn't have a clue what he meant. Not until now."

Lucas shrugged and tilted his head, then tightened something else with an even smaller tool.

"Did I also mention that he'd asked Brianna to marry him when she was dying?" She fingered the spine of the yearbook.

Lucas pulled in his chin. "Really."

Her eyes welled up. "And he would have married her, too, if she'd lived. Then he let me leave without ever coming after me. I was so sure he would. He broke my heart so many times that I just couldn't take it anymore." She palmed her cheeks to remove a fresh batch of tears. "The thing is, I never quit loving him, and…"

"Then why not move back here and be with him?"

Why did men always make complicated things sound so simple? "I have a job and responsibilities in Portland."

"And you've got your family and a man to love right here in Whispering Oaks. Do the math, genius."

"Ugh. It's not that easy."

"Sure it is. What do you have in Portland that you can't find here?"

What *did* she have in Portland that could really compare with home? Lucas was right. Her family was here, her roots…and Jack.

She picked up the book and thumbed through the pages, spotting a picture of herself as a bony teen here and there. And there was Jack. Even then he was buff— for a hundred-and-forty pounder. She smiled. And there was Brianna, pretty and fragile-looking, wearing the trendiest clothes. She flipped through more pages and a small note dropped out. Her pulse sprinted a few beats when she recognized the tiny creased square of white—a note from Jack from the pre-leukemia days. She opened it to find familiar handwriting.

*Speedy, you're the one for me. Love, Jack.*

History couldn't be changed, and wise people learned from it. Jack was meant to be in her life. Denying that truth had stunted her growth for years. Sitting in her brother's Mustang, reminiscing about the rough old days, wondering how to handle the future, she reread the note and sure as hell didn't need any more proof.

"Do you believe in people finding the love of their life, Lucas?"

"Nope. But maybe in your case..."

She'd found Jack again after all these years. Her feelings for him were as strong now as they'd been in eleventh grade, more so after being with him this past month, after getting to know him all over again, realizing how sweet and considerate he was, and especially after making love with him. Damn, she could never have imagined something that wonderful. He'd asked one thing of her, to move past all the confusion and heartache that Brianna's illness and death had brought. Well, it was long overdue to *finally* move forward.

She closed her eyes and hugged the yearbook, making one last decision.

Now that she'd rediscovered Jackson Lightfoot, she was sure as hell not going to lose him again. Ever.

She got out of the car, determined to find him tomorrow and tell him that she loved him and could never think of loving anyone else. Sure she'd have to work things out at the clinic, give notice, help them find her replacement, let her lease go and whatever else. That is, if after the grief she'd given him the other night, he still wanted her.

She closed the car door. "Thanks for listening, little brother. Looks like I owe you another one."

His smile, through tired yet radiating eyes, gave her all the encouragement she needed.

"And by the way, when you get ready to find the love of your life, may I suggest that you start by looking next door?"

He threw a greasy rag at her on her way out of the garage. Anne knew she was right, and prayed it wouldn't take him as long to figure it out as it had for her with Jack.

With new determination, she strode back to the house. She needed to catch a couple hours of sleep, though she doubted she'd be able to. When daylight rose, she'd shower and dress, and find a way to let her man know exactly how she felt.

Jack sat rubbing his shoulder in the triage area at the mobile command post. "I'm fine, really. I just got knocked over by a falling branch. Look, I'm not even bruised."

He moved both of his arms and neck to demonstrate that he hadn't sustained any injuries.

"Your crew said you'd passed out."

"Not true. It knocked the wind out of me. I was stunned, that's all."

"Take off your shirt. Let me have a look," said the EMT.

Jack did what he was told, and let the guy put his

arm and shoulder through several range of motion maneuvers. He gritted his teeth when the EMT pressed into one particular tender area on back.

"Looks like you've bruised your trapezius." He put an ice pack on his shoulder. "Keep it iced down today. Tomorrow, use some heat."

Jack nodded and accepted the anti-inflammatories the guy handed him. He washed them down with half a bottle of water.

Threads of early morning light spun through the smoke-filled sky. Exhaustion made him too tired to talk further. He sat on the bench watching the mobile command unit with everyone scuttling about. More guys just like him pushed to their limits, but continuing on duty because a job had to be done.

The absence of wind had made their jobs more routine and significantly easier.

"We've got seventy-percent containment," he heard someone say.

Amazing. Yesterday the fire had total control. Today, well, maybe all of their efforts wouldn't be for naught.

What a difference a day made when Mother Nature was on your side and reinforcements had arrived.

Today—was one day closer to when Anne would leave. He didn't want to let her do it. He loved her. But if he loved her, he needed to understand that she had her job in Portland, and she had to go back.

When he was a kid and his mother left, he didn't have the power to stop her. And when nothing the doctors did could cure Brianna, again he was powerless.

But with Anne, he didn't have to let it happen. He didn't have to lie down and let life walk over him anymore. He'd do whatever it took to make her his. He'd be willing to be with her wherever she wanted to be. If she wanted to live in Portland, hell, he'd find work as a teacher there. If she'd have him, he'd do anything to make it work. All she had to do was say the words he'd been waiting to hear since he was seventeen.

"You're relieved from duty, Lightfoot. Go home. Get some rest."

He stood and shook hands with his unit leader.

"Thanks. I won't argue with you."

"Good job, man. We've finally got this bad boy under control." The middle-aged man glanced toward the sky. "As long as the wind backs off, we'll be fine. We're transporting some guys back to the fire station. They'll be leaving in a few minutes. Gather up your gear and get the hell out of here."

Covered in ash and feeling wasted, Jack welcomed the idea of heading home. He needed sleep so he'd have enough energy to fight for the one person he loved.

He tossed the ice pack into the trash and put his T-shirt back on, letting the suspenders from his Nomex pants hang at his sides. With his work boots feeling like they were filled with bricks, and his jacket under his arm, he walked toward the transportation vehicle loading a few of the other guys.

Down the canyon a group of curious bystanders gathered behind the cordoned-off barriers. He saw a woman's silhouette in the early morning light. She was

taller than average, like Anne, and had the same body
build...and hair to her shoulders.

*It* is *Anne.*

Already dehydrated, his mouth suddenly felt as dry
as charred bark.

Was she here to say goodbye?

She broke away from the group and rushed toward
him.

Anne saw the fireman coming toward her. Chills
of excitement poured over her skin, and her stomach
filled with fluttering wings of anticipation. His hat sat
cocked back on his forehead making him look even
more handsome. Under the soot and dirt, accentuating
all the lines and angles, she recognized every feature
of the man she loved.

He must have recognized her, too, because he picked
up his pace. "Anne?" he called out.

Through the black smudges covering his face, she
focused on the one feature she'd loved since she'd been
fifteen—his fern green eyes. On the dusty road from
the command post, with plumes of dirty air hanging in
the sky, those eyes called out to her like a lighthouse
beacon guiding her home.

"Jack!"

As Anne came closer to Jack, the wan smile on her
face and tears in her eyes looked like a typical reaction to the smoke, but he knew better. He rushed closer
needing to be near her. Her expression looked pained,

as if she had heart-wrenching news. *She better not be leaving today, she wouldn't be that cruel.*

She sprinted toward him and threw her arms around him. Her weight and warmth felt like heaven, and she sure as hell didn't feel like a woman bearing bad news. He dropped his jacket to hold her tighter. Nothing in his life had ever felt better than Anne in his arms.

She kissed him, smashing her lips onto his. He kissed her back. Ashes and sweat mingled together making everything taste like salt and charred lips, but he didn't care, especially since beneath everything was the sweet, sweet taste of Anne. She was here in his arms with her mouth on his—she couldn't be bringing bad news.

Anne pulled back, and he smiled. Ash smudges rimmed her mouth and dotted the tip of her nose, making hers the most beautiful face he'd ever seen. He had to tell her how he felt before she said anything about leaving. He couldn't let her go without her knowing how he felt.

"I love you," he said at the exact moment she said, "I love you, Jack."

She loved him. She loved him! Ready to burst, he laughed and hugged her, and her cinnamon gum kisses quickly wiped out the smoke and ash memories. Now that he'd heard those fantastic words, even though dead tired, all he wanted was to be physically connected to her.

"Let me take you home," she said, forehead to forehead.

"That's the best invitation I've ever heard," he said, kissing her cheek, adding more smudges to her collection.

Anne led Jack up the steps to his town house and inside—his dirty face had never looked more handsome.

"Let me get cleaned up," he said, dropping his gear in a pile on the entryway tile.

He made a move for the hall but she grabbed his wrist. "I could use a shower, too."

The contrast between his devastatingly white smile and the ash and dirt on his face made her knees wobble.

"Then let's go, speedy."

They lost their clothes in record time. The bathroom filled up with steam and steamy looks. Jack's muscles seemed more cut than before, probably from all the hard labor he'd been doing the last few days. His near concave stomach was more proof he'd been underfed, and from the half-hooded and heated stare he gave her, food seemed to be the last thing on his mind. She hadn't even touched him, yet he was erect, showing no sign of a man who'd been overworked and probably hadn't slept in two days.

Her body responded in every way, but there was something else. Powerful feelings spilled out from inside, they twirled and twisted throughout every cell. Jack knew she loved him and he loved her, and that was the craziest aphrodisiac of all.

He took her wrist and led her inside the shower.

They lathered, hugged and cuddled, and washed more, mixing business with pleasure. She found the beginnings of a large bruise on his shoulder and traced it with her fingertips, knowing when the time was right he'd tell her how it had happened. Not now. Not while they showered and washed each other. She gave his shoulder a quick and gentle kiss. In between each pass of the soap, they kissed. Before each turn for one to wash the other's back, they kissed more. And before and after rinsing under the running water, they kissed again. Water forced its way into their hungry kisses, but didn't begin to dilute their passion.

Finally they stood flush together; slick skin to slick skin, caressing and holding each other, sending sparks of heat deep inside Anne. Jack lifted her, as he had once before, and she knew the perfect position to help him enter her. He leaned her up against the cold tile, giving her an unexpected thrill, and rocked her over his erection. She let go of every inhibition, allowing him to take her to that place only he could. He took his time, seeming to savor the sensation and enjoying it as much as she did.

He watched her when he wasn't kissing her. She let him see how he made her feel. She had nothing left to hide from Jack.

A little noise caught in her throat as he took her to the edge, and a sudden change in temperature from hot to cold from outlasting the water heater added a running jump to her final freefall. Dare Devil's Drop, all over again. Without interruption, he turned off the shower, and was right there with her, diving over the cliff, his head buried in her neck....

A few minutes later, Jack toweled off Anne as she shivered, only then realizing how cold things had gotten. He stood behind her and wrapped his arms around her chest adding his body heat to hers, kissing her neck, starting a whole new string of tingling chills. She didn't know how she'd survived all these years without knowing him this way. And every fantasy she'd ever conjured up hadn't come close to this reality.

"I love you," he said.

"I love you, too."

He walked her into the bedroom and pulled back the covers on the bed. They crawled inside and cuddled close together. She knew he needed to sleep, and she had a million plans to make. While he slept, she'd lie beside him, watching him and pinch herself from time to time so she'd know it wasn't all a dream.

Once Jack had settled into the warm covers, and Anne rested her head on his shoulder, he stroked her hair, ran his fingers through the ends, separated and dropped the tendrils, as if he'd never explored anything like it. She loved the feathery fan tickling her neck, and she smiled against his chest. He lifted her chin and kissed her—a sweet, soft, good-night lover's kiss. His warmth spread like butter over her skin, soothing and smoothing out the last of her tension. Midkiss, oozing with contentment, something extra special happened. She couldn't deny what she'd never felt before this melding of their lips—the *I'll-be-here-when-you-*

*wake* kiss felt like it came with nothing short of a life-time guarantee. And though logically she knew nothing in life could be guaranteed, she savored this moment with the man she loved.

After one last sigh, Anne snuggled into Jack's chest and feeling like she'd finally found her way home, she fell asleep.

The delectable aroma of coffee and cocoa lured Anne from her deep and contented sleep. She rolled onto her back and inched open her eyelids to see Jack standing at the foot of the bed wearing a special *that's-right,-I'm-the-guy-who-rocked-your-world* look.

"Hi," she said, pushing her tangled hair from her face. He held two large red mugs.

"Hey." He covered the distance in three steps and sat facing her. "I never made you that mocha cappuccino I promised," he said, handing her one of the cups.

She sat up, wrapping the sheet across her chest. "It smells heavenly. Oh, look, you've even made a little picture in the froth." It was a heart, and it made hers clench.

"Yeah, well, I had to learn how to do it when I took the barista job." He raised his eyebrows. "I never ever thought it would come in handy until now." His bright eyes crinkled as he gave a self-deprecating smile.

She took a sip, her gaze on Jack. "Hmm, delicious." *And so are you.*

There he was, shirtless, taut chest and stomach, in a

pair of navy blue, thigh-length Jockey briefs. His eyes didn't waver. "We need to talk."

She blew on her steamy brew. "That's an understatement."

Jack took a long draw from his mug, pressed his lips together briefly and nailed her with his stare. "I gave you an ultimatum."

She nodded, midsip. "Yes, you did."

"Jocelyn told me that you're leaving tomorrow, so what am I supposed to think?"

"I promise I'm not running away, I planned to talk to you before I left, Jack. Even before we said…"

"I love you?" His brows lifted ever so slightly.

"Yes." She set her cup on the bedside table. "I love you. And I do, but I promised I'd be back at work on Monday. I've been gone over a month. It's a new job. You understand." She searched his eyes for a glimmer of acceptance.

"I don't want you to go, but I'm not unreasonable." He put his cup beside hers and nudged into bed next to her, under the blanket. He was the most reasonable man she'd ever met. "So we've got to work this out now."

He lay facing her, elbow bent, his head propped up by his hand.

"You've got to finish out the semester teaching," she said, trying not to lose her train of thought while staring into his eyes.

"And you've got an apartment lease, and a job." He traced her lower lip with his thumb.

"You love Whispering Oaks."

"And you love Portland."

She nodded.

"So what do you suggest we do?" He lifted her chin. "Draw straws?"

He chuckled. "I'll fly up to Portland every other weekend."

"And I'll fly home every other weekend."

He glanced down and to the right, inhaling a long breath. "I laid it all on the line to you the other night at the beach. It's time to forget and move on. I don't want to look back anymore."

"No rehashing what we can't change," she said. "I get it. No more guilt trips. That's our history." She touched his cheek. "This is our future."

He cupped her neck, fingers delving into her hair. "Are you ready to leave it all behind? To be with me?"

"I understand why you did what you did, Jack. Bri needed hope to live. Consider the subject dropped." She grasped his forearm. "And I promise I'll never leave you, I'll never run away. From now on it's only you, me and our future."

He brushed her cheek with his knuckles and looked into her eyes, overwhelming her with a sincere, fern green stare. "I'll live where you want, I'm sick of living without you."

A weight lifted off her chest, allowing her to take her deepest breath in what seemed like forever. He gave her the choice to live wherever she wanted, and she knew exactly where that was. "Oh, Jack," she said, tears brimming in her eyes. "It doesn't matter where we live. I can give notice and look for a job here."

"Only if that's what you really want to do, because I can find a job in Portland, too." His gaze moved back and forth between each of her eyes. She knew beyond a doubt he meant it.

"Ever since I left home, I've been trying to make myself fit in someplace I really didn't belong."

"Not that I'm pressuring you or anything, but I'm pretty sure I know exactly where you belong." Their gazes fused. "Right here in Whispering Oaks with me...and your family."

A tiny ironic laugh slipped from between her lips. "I've wasted so much time and energy denying it."

"That you belong to me?"

She grinned. "Oh, Jack, I've belonged to you since I was sixteen."

A welcoming smile stretched slowly across his lips. "I knew you used to tag along for a reason."

She blurted out a laugh, snatched the pillow behind her and whacked him with it. He grabbed both of her wrists and pulled her close for a kiss. Just before their lips met, another pillow, an old pillow with a particular embroidered saying, popped into her mind.

Jack's warm kiss melted away the last of Anne's resistance. *Bye-bye negative old memories. I forgive myself. Hello new life.*

He eased her back onto the pillow, and she wrapped her arms around his neck pulling him home.

"What's your take on September?" he asked.

"September?"

"Yeah. I always thought it would be a nice month to get married."

*Well, what do you know. Grandma was right—good things really do come for those who wait.*

* * * * *

# HEART & HOME

Heartwarming romances where love can
happen right when you least expect it.

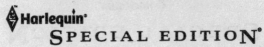

## SPECIAL EDITION®

### COMING NEXT MONTH
### AVAILABLE MARCH 27, 2012

**#2179 A COLD CREEK REUNION**
*The Cowboys of Cold Creek*
**RaeAnne Thayne**

**#2180 THE PRINCE'S SECRET BABY**
*The Bravo Royales*
**Christine Rimmer**

**#2181 FORTUNE'S HERO**
*The Fortunes of Texas: Whirlwind Romance*
**Susan Crosby**

**#2182 HAVING ADAM'S BABY**
*Welcome to Destiny*
**Christyne Butler**

**#2183 HUSBAND FOR A WEEKEND**
**Gina Wilkins**

**#2184 THE DOCTOR'S NOT-SO-LITTLE
SECRET**
*Rx for Love*
**Cindy Kirk**

# REQUEST YOUR FREE BOOKS!
## 2 FREE NOVELS PLUS 2 FREE GIFTS!

# SPECIAL EDITION
## Life, Love & Family

# PRESENTING...

## *More Than Words*

### STORIES OF THE HEART

*Three bestselling authors*
*Three real-life heroines*

Even as you read these words, there are women just like you stepping up and making a difference in their communities, making our world a better place to live. Three such exceptional women have been selected as recipients of Harlequin's More Than Words award. To celebrate their accomplishments, three bestselling authors have written short stories inspired by these real-life heroines.

Proceeds from the sale of this book will be reinvested into the Harlequin More Than Words program to support causes that are of concern to women.

### Visit

# www.HarlequinMoreThanWords.com

to nominate a real-life heroine from your community.

www.Harlequin.com

*Taft Bowman knew he'd ruined any chance he'd had for happiness with Laura Pendleton when he drove her away years ago...and into the arms of another man, thousands of miles away. Now she was back, a widow with two small children...and despite himself, he was starting to believe in second chances.*

*Harlequin Special® Edition® presents a new installment in USA TODAY bestselling author RaeAnne Thayne's miniseries,*
THE COWBOYS OF COLD CREEK.

*Enjoy a sneak peek of*
*A COLD CREEK REUNION*

*Available April 2012 from Harlequin® Special Edition®*

A younger woman stood there, and from this distance he had only a strange impression, as though she was somehow standing on an island of calm amid the chaos of the scene, the flashing lights of the emergency vehicles, shouts between his crew members, the excited buzz of the crowd.

And then the woman turned and he just about tripped over a snaking fire hose somebody shouldn't have left there.

Laura.

He froze, and for the first time in fifteen years as a firefighter, he forgot about the incident, his mission, just what the hell he was doing here.

Laura.

Ten years. He hadn't seen her in all that time, since the week before their wedding when she had given him back his ring and left town. Not just town. She had left the whole damn country, as if she couldn't run far enough to get away from him.

Some part of him desperately wanted to think he had made some kind of mistake. It couldn't be her. That was just some other slender woman with a long sweep of honey-blond hair and big, blue, unforgettable eyes. But no. It was definitely Laura. Sweet and lovely.

Not his.

He was going to have to go over there and talk to her. He didn't want to. He wanted to stand there and pretend he hadn't seen her. But he was the fire chief. He couldn't hide out just because he had a painful history with the daughter of the property owner.

Sometimes he hated his job.

*Will Taft and Laura be able to make the years recede...or is the gulf between them too broad to ever cross?*

*Find out in*
*A COLD CREEK REUNION*
*Available April 2012 from Harlequin® Special Edition®*
*wherever books are sold.*

Celebrate the 30th anniversary
of Harlequin® Special Edition® with a bonus story
included in each Special Edition® book in April!

**Harlequin® Romance**

*Get swept away with a brand-new miniseries*
*by* **USA TODAY** *bestselling author*

# MARGARET WAY

## *The Langdon Dynasty*

Amelia Norton knows that in order to embrace her future,
she must first face her past. As she unravels her family's secrets,
she is forced to turn to gorgeous cattleman Dev Langdon for
support—the man she vowed never to fall for again.

Against the haze of the sweltering Australian heat Mel's
guarded exterior begins to crumble…and Dev will do
whatever it takes to convince his childhood sweetheart
to be his bride.

### THE CATTLE KING'S BRIDE
*Available April 2012*

### And look for
### ARGENTINIAN IN THE OUTBACK
*Coming in May 2012*

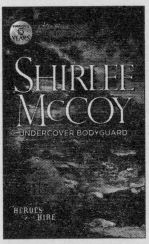